STRIPPED

MARRIED TO THE MAFIA BOOK 1

A.G. KHALIQ

LIMITLESS
PUBLISHING

Limitless Publishing, LLC

Kailua, HI 96734

www.limitlesspublishing.com

Formatting: Limitless Publishing, LLC

Cover Design: Deranged Doctor Design

ISBN-13: 978-1-954194-20-5

For Samreen.
Thank you for being an amazing friend
and always being there for me. x

ACKNOWLEDGMENTS

Thank you to the Limitless Publishing team for making my dreams of having a book deal come true.

Thank you to my editor, Toni Rakestraw, for your help with perfecting this novel.

PROLOGUE

Raven

$\mathcal{M}$y heart was pounding against my chest as I lay in the hospital bed, my lungs constricting.

I feared for my life. I took a deep breath in...and a deep breath out.

A deep breath in...and a deep breath out, doing my best to remain strong for my unborn child. Doing my best to fight this monster, and not let him get the better of me. Doing my best to keep going...even though it was proving to be more and more difficult.

"You think that just because you're outside of my home you can open that mouth of yours, you bitch?" he snarled, making his way to my bed.

"*You belong to me!*" he bellowed. "You thought you could speak to the police about what I did to you?"

He cracked up with laughter, a menacing laugh that caused my head to sear.

"You don't know I pay off the police to keep me out of jail?" he sneered. "You really thought you could get rid of me? You will never get rid of me. *Never!*"

He spat on me, clambering on top of me, slapping my face to the side, forcing me to look him in his eyes.

Before he began punching me mercilessly, I could feel my jaw snap as he continued to beat me. Not stopping for a breath. Not sparing me any mercy.

I faded in and out of unconsciousness as the pain began to overwhelm my body.

Limp, bruised and bloody.

My surroundings blurred around me. I did my best to speak, but I could barely let out a sound as he wrapped his hands around my neck, squeezing for all he was worth.

"P-Please, no!" I breathed. "You're going to kill my baby!"

Tears rolled down my cheeks as he let go of my neck, a smirk forming on the corner of his lips.

"P-Please, it hurts too much..." I struggled, but it just came out as a murmur.

"I loved you and you went against me!" he roared, shaking his fists with anger as his veins pulsated their way to the surface of his skin. "You won't walk out of this hospital alive."

And those were the last words I heard...*before everything went black.*

RAVEN

"No..." I screamed as I jolted upward from my sleep. "No, no, no!"

I began sweating profusely as I did my best to regain consciousness. The moon was out, glimmering against the window of my cheap, worn-out apartment, my torn curtains barely covering the view. There was no doubt I wasn't in the hospital, pregnant with a baby, fearing for my life from the monster in my dreams...

I was in my own bedroom, in my own home.

I was *safe*.

I didn't know why I kept having these weird dreams. These dreams of a man attacking me, possessing me, wanting to kill me. Nightmares of an abusive man holding a choke-hold over my life...

When in reality, I was lonely, and I didn't even have a boyfriend. My life was just working, day in and day out, and then coming home to my apartment, having just my sister for company.

I rubbed my eyes groggily, reaching for my phone on the

bedside table. I gasped in shock as I read the time on the phone, which was ten p.m.

"I'm gonna be late for work!" I screamed angrily.

This wasn't good...

This wasn't good *at all.*

I needed to quickly get ready, because my boss was going to be mad at me for being late. Boss despised me and treated me like shit, and this would only add more fuel to the fire. I was supposed to be at the club over an hour ago.

I quickly tumbled out of bed, tidying my hair in the mirror, and putting on some leggings and a crop top. I didn't have time to do my makeup or check for a proper outfit—I needed to set off straight away.

"This will have to do," I muttered to myself, exhausted, and then began making my way out of my bedroom.

I saw my sister Sophia sitting on the couch with her legs up, watching the television. She was blonde, pretty, with bright blue eyes, and pale skin.

"Hey Sophia, I'm gonna go to work now, babe," I informed her.

"Stay safe from the creeps at the bar," she replied with a smile, before reaching for the television remote to change the channel.

I chuckled in response, amused.

"I will, don't stay up too late, babe." I grinned.

She nodded at me, absorbing herself into watching *Prison Break*. I gave her a small smile before I headed to my car, locking the door behind me.

Before I knew it, I was driving down the motorway in London at high speed. I felt bad for lying to my sister, but I was too ashamed to tell her where I really worked.

Too ashamed to tell her that I was a *stripper*.

She was too young, and I didn't want her to get involved in these things at her age. She was still a teenager, and I was in my twenties. I couldn't let her into this disgusting world…

It was for the best.

I didn't want this life for her. I was only doing it for the money in the hope that one day, things would get better for us, and we wouldn't have to keep living on the bare minimum in a council estate, in an area full of crime.

Sophia could never follow in my footsteps. I wanted her to go through a proper education. To have the chance to succeed, and get the best shot at life.

The chance that I never had.

* * *

I ARRIVED at the strip club, leaving my car in the car park. I made my way inside, the loud music roaring in my ears. I searched around the area, doing my best to figure out where Boss was. It was really busy today, and there were so many clients here. Men in their sixties getting lap dances, the strippers getting money thrown on them while they ground their hips against the men's bodies. I locked my eyes with Polly, one of the strippers I knew here. The man was rubbing her ass with his hand, and she looked really uncomfortable. I felt terrible for her. Touching was never meant to be a part of this line of work, just dancing, but obviously, some disgusting men just couldn't help themselves…

"You're late, you bitch!" came a roaring voice, causing me to jolt upwards and snap out of my thoughts. I turned around, my heart hammering against my chest, only to realise I was standing face-to-face with Boss. He'd found me…

And he looked ready to murder.

"You've got some nerve turning up here an hour late, I pay your fucking wages," he barked angrily, rattling his fists.

"I've had ten men waiting for a performance since eight o'clock. You're losing me too much goddamn money!"

I did my best to swallow down a lump that had caught in my throat, my eyes brimming with tears. I bit my lip to stop the tears from falling, feeling angry and humiliated, my insides twisting into knots. I should have been used to this treatment by now, but whenever Boss spoke to me like this, like I was a dog, a rabid animal, it always tipped me over the edge.

"I'm really sorry, Boss, I had to take care of some things..." I stumbled, doing my best to rectify the situation.

"I don't wanna hear your lousy excuses," he snarled, cutting me off. "I'd fire you on the spot, but the regulars have taken quite a liking to you." He rolled his eyes. "So instead, you'll be punished. The money will be deducted from your wages, and you'll have to do unpaid overtime."

I drew out a deep breath, shaking my head, feeling defeated. I was so tired of having my wages cut, when the only reason I was doing this job was because of how desperate I was for the money. It was always a sting to the chest whenever Boss didn't pay me enough. It was hard enough for me to get by as it was.

"And how many times have I told you to get changed before you come into my club?" he sighed, shaking his head at my outfit. "Fucking hell, Raven, just get out of my damn sight."

I quickly rubbed my eyes, doing my best to dry my tears and get myself together. I had to get my head back in the game if I was going to survive work tonight. It was a busy night, so it was one of the most important for collecting tips. I would be better off just doing as I was told.

I made my way to the changing rooms, feeling stupid for not coming in the right outfit and makeup. I should have just done it at home rather than having to waste time doing it here…I always behaved hastily under pressure.

I quickly threw on a tight red mini-dress which emphasized my cleavage, slim waist, and round ass, and put on some red lipstick and lipgloss onto my plump lips. This would have to do.

I let out a sigh I didn't know I was holding as I stared back at my reflection in the dressing room. My dark brown hair fell past my shoulders, my dark brown eyes were blood-shot and watery. My milky brown skin looked tired and exhausted. I could hardly recognise myself anymore. It was like I was staring back at a complete stranger. This wasn't the way life was supposed to go. This wasn't what I was destined to do for all my life. There had to be more to life than *this*…

I shook my head before turning on my heel, and made my way to the stage to join the other strippers. I started dancing seductively against the pole, wrapping my legs around it, doing my best to put on a good show, even though I had bile in my throat whenever I saw the men stare at me with their perverted glances.

"WOOOHOOOO!" came the cheers of the crowd as I took my dress off so I was just in my lingerie, a transparent bralette and a thong.

I wished I didn't have to do this job.

I had to work at a coffee shop in the daytime too, just to make ends meet.

I had to look after my sister on my own with nobody else in the picture, and that's why I struggled so hard. No mother, no father, no proper friends, no other siblings.

I had a really rough childhood.

That childhood brought me to where I was today.

Dancing naked in front of a bunch of perverted men, getting money thrown at me only for my boss to take it all.

Getting my wages cut over the smallest mistakes.

Getting harassed by creeps at the club, trying to touch me inappropriately and get sexual favors.

I didn't want to do it, but Boss insisted I never fought any of the men, because them getting what they wanted meant more money for the business.

I was trapped with no way out.

This was the only life I knew, and for all I knew, this was the only life I was ever going to lead.

Nothing was ever going to get better for me.

I was *sure* of it.

But I suddenly found myself rubbing my chin in thought, mesmerized, as my eyes locked with a man in the crowd. A man who had unexpectedly entered the club, and looked like the last man who would come to a place like this. He looked out of place, foreign, almost like he didn't belong here.

A man with dark brown hair, pale hazel eyes, a rough, scruffy beard, and light brown skin. He was wearing a black jacket with a shirt that was half unbuttoned, revealing a skull tattoo across his chest...

And he wouldn't take his eyes off of me for one moment.

Every part of him screamed power, dominance, fearlessness. His presence radiated the room.

Who was this man that had just entered the club?

RAVEN

This man looked incredibly intimidating.

     I felt uncomfortable dancing almost naked with him watching me.

I just wanted to hide.

I could feel my insides swimming with nerves, not wanting to stay on stage for a minute longer. I almost felt ashamed and embarrassed that this man had to see me like this. He looked powerful, and he would probably see me as a cheap whore. People always made assumptions about people and judged what they didn't know before they even got to know a person...

And I knew this man was probably doing the same.

I suddenly felt sick to my stomach, my insides twisting into knots. I didn't want to humiliate myself. There was something about this man, and the way he held his gaze with mine...

I knew if I stayed here, continuing to watch him stare at me, I would feel even more worse than I already did. I needed to get out of here, and fast. I needed to get away before he approached me, because I knew that nothing good would come out of it. I needed him to stop looking at me.

I quickly slipped my mini-dress back on before I made my way off the stage.

"Great performance, sweet cheeks," a man said. He wolf-whistled, and spun me around, tossing one hundred dollars at me. His arm moved to my waist, but I quickly slapped it off, walking away as fast as I could, leaving him cursing and pissed off.

I pushed through the crowd and made my way to the bar, suddenly needing a drink. I was angry, my blood boiling to the surface. I was angry that people saw me as a whore when I was a pure woman, and had never slept with a man willingly. I was doing this job to stop me and my sister from going hungry and being homeless...

Not because I was *easy*.

I allowed the liquor to burn down my throat as I continued to sip from the cup. I wished it would make me feel better and help me calm down.

But I just felt worse and worse.

"Why aren't you performing?" roared a voice.

I spun around to see that Boss had followed me again. The man couldn't even leave me in peace for two minutes without complaining at me endlessly and biting me in the ass.

"Didn't I explain to you that you were being punished, goddammit?" he bellowed angrily.

"Yes, Boss..." I stumbled shakily, swallowing down a lump in my throat as I slammed my drink down back onto the bar table. "I was just taking a break..."

I could feel my eyes prick with tears, not wanting to go back to the stage to dance, especially after I'd seen that man in the crowd.

"Can't I just serve drinks today?" I pleaded.

Boss slapped my face, and my hand leapt to my face in shock. I couldn't believe it.

I couldn't fucking believe it...

"First you turn up late, then you have the audacity to take a break when you've hardly done any work?" he snarled. "Stay in your lane, you whore. Get back to work." His voice dropped to barely above a whisper, and I knew he meant business, and that I shouldn't argue with him. He'd hardly ever raised his hands to me before...

Things were only going to get worse for me if I defied him.

I could feel silent tears roll down my cheeks, even though I did my best to hold them back. I couldn't believe he slapped me.

This bastard...

How *dare* he.

My heart hammered against my chest, my breathing labored. I took several deep breaths in and out, doing my best to regain my composure. I knew it wouldn't benefit me if I made a scene or argued back.

It was either putting up with this or having to live on the streets...

I had to keep reminding myself of that whenever things got too tough.

"Okay, Boss, I'll get back right away," I mumbled.

"Okay, good. I have a man who wants a private dance, and he's willing to pay a lot of cash," he hissed matter-of-factly, getting straight down to business. "Make sure you do everything he says. You're not screwing this up."

Make sure you do everything he says...

His words replayed themselves over and over to me, like a form of torture. Etching themselves into my memory. I knew this wasn't good...

It meant if this man wanted to touch me, I would have to allow him...

I could feel my heart in my throat, feeling too weak and exhausted to fight back. I just wanted to get this night over with, and then go home to my bed. The sooner I got this over with, the better.

"Okay..." I breathed.

"Ready to go, sunshine?" came a voice.

I looked up to see the man who wanted the private dance. He was an old man in his sixties, and he was wearing an olive green sweater, paired with light olive-colored trousers. He had pleated grey hair and grey eyes, and a wrinkly face. Blood continued to pound through my body, sizzling to the point that it felt like I had no fight left.

"Y-Yes," I managed timidly, shaking my head.

The creep nodded, making his way out of the bar to the private lounge, and I followed him, sick churning in my stomach.

From the corner of my eye, I could have sworn that the same mesmerizing man from the crowd was still watching me. Watching me follow this old, creepy man...

But I figured it was just my mind playing tricks on me.

* * *

"OKAY, sexy...show me what you got." The creep smiled, sitting down on the couch, bopping his head forward in anticipation. His predatory eyes smoldered with lust and darkened with desire as he drunk me in, staring at my body. Bile churned in my throat. I wasn't looking forward to this at all.

I pleaded with my body to move and start dancing. To start putting on a show for this bastard so I could just take my money and leave. But I felt frozen to the spot, suddenly barely able to move. Not being able to shift my limbs a single bit, and I didn't know why. My body was pounding with fear.

The creep stared at me agitatedly, getting tired of waiting. He folded his arms angrily, unimpressed.

"Come on, why aren't you dancing?" he snapped, rattling his fists impatiently.

"I—" I stammered.

"What?" he barked, furrowing his eyebrows, getting up on his feet, and stepping closer to me. I backed away from him slowly, feeling my eyes well with tears.

"I can't do this," I croaked.

The corners of his mouth formed into a frown, and he was no longer smiling. He looked pissed off, angry...

Almost *dangerous.*

I didn't know what was wrong with me today. I was doing nothing my boss was asking of me.

I'd reached breaking point, and I couldn't do this anymore. I couldn't keep living my life like this. Being treated as a lapdog, being treated as an animal.

Being treated as a slave for my motherfucking boss.

Not being able to have a say in anything. Not being able to be my own woman. To make my own choices. To break free from the chains of my life.

The only image I had in my head was of the man I had just seen in the club.

The way he was looking at me, with so much interest and curiosity.

The way his eyes were piercing mine.

"Come on, don't be like this," the creep encouraged, doing his best to egg me on. "It would be a shame for me to have come all this way for nothing. Your boss made me a lot of promises...and if those promises aren't fulfilled, let's just say, there'll be trouble for both of you."

"Sorry, sir, but I have the right to refuse anything I don't want to do," I mumbled in my own defence, swallowing. "If you have a problem you can go somewhere else, or ask somebody else for a dance."

He cracked up with laughter, looking amused, like he wasn't taking me seriously. I stared back at him with an uneasy expression on my face, because I had no idea of what this man was capable of. I could feel my heart pound in fear. I'd never stood up for myself like this before...

I guessed that was why people treated me like trash.

"I can make it worth your while, babe. I can make you rich, you'll never need money again." He smirked, biting his finger in anticipation.

He still didn't understand the fact that *no* meant *no*. *No* didn't mean that he should carry on persuading me to agree.

"Sorry, sir, no," I repeated firmly.

He folded his arms angrily, his veins suddenly pulsing their way to the surface of his skin. His pupils dilated, as if I were staring back at a *monster*. A fucking beast.

"You think you have a choice?" he said quietly, his low voice causing me to jolt upwards as I began sweating profusely. "You dare to say no to me, you whore?"

I stepped backwards, mortified, suddenly terrified of the man was standing before me. He looked like he wanted to murder.

"W-What...what are you gonna do?" I cried out.

"You will sleep with me, whether you like it or not!" he demanded, grabbing hold of my arm with such a force that I almost tripped. I could feel my life flash before my eyes as he began tugging on my clothes.

I couldn't let this happen...

I couldn't let this fucking happen.

"No...*no!*" I screamed.

"Shut your mouth!" he growled, leaning in for a kiss.

As he did this, I took the opportunity to kick him hard in the crotch with my high heels. He cried out in pain, clutching his privates.

I ran as fast as I could. As fast as my legs would move.

I bolted through the crowd in the club, and Boss caught my glance, with murder written all over his face.

"Where the hell do you think you're going?" he called out after me, screaming angrily. *"Come back inside right now!"*

I ignored his screams, allowing them to fade into the loud music. I wanted to forget reality for a while. Wanted to forget that this was my life.

Wanted out, even if it was just for one night.

I had to keep running. I didn't want to face Boss tonight. I didn't want to have to go back into the private lounge with that bastard, and be forced to do things I didn't want to do.

I didn't want this life anymore.

My eyes grew hazy as my surroundings blurred around me. Before I knew it, I was in an alleyway near the club, and I had no idea where I should go, or which way I should turn.

"I need to get out of here before Boss finds me!" I cried out. "I'm in big trouble!"

I bent down and clutched my chest in agony, doing my best to regain my strength because my feet were searing in pain from running in these high heels. As my heart-rate started to return to normal, and I slowly moved my eyes back upwards, I was greeted by the last person I expected to see here.

The mesmerizing man from the crowd was standing before me in the alleyway, his arms folded, with a look of genuine concern on his face. I couldn't believe my eyes.

What the hell was he doing here?

"I'm Lazarus," he said quietly. "Come with me. I'll take you to safety."

I swallowed a lump in my throat, not knowing why this man wanted to help me.

But I also knew I had no choice but to put my trust in a total stranger...

Because my life depended on it.

RAVEN

$\mathcal{I}$ gave him a timid nod, hardly able to get any words out. Hardly able to string a sentence together, because my throat suddenly felt dry.

"He'll catch up in a few minutes. Go hide somewhere, and I'll speak to him and throw him off the trail so he doesn't find you," said Lazarus.

"O-Okay," I breathed.

I looked around, and noticed some dustbins at the back of the alley. I quickly crept behind one, allowing the massive bins to conceal me. My heart pounded against my chest. I knew I would be dead meat if my boss found me here, especially after defying him. I didn't want to learn what he was capable of.

He'd already treated me so harshly over me just making small mistakes.

Blood roared in my ears as I made silent prayers to God in my head, praying to Him to protect me. Thanking Him for sending this Lazarus character to help me. I just hoped that Lazarus would be able to keep Boss at bay.

I took a peek around the bin, and saw Boss standing there

with Lazarus. My heart leapt to my throat as I quickly slid back into position, making sure I was hidden properly.

"Hey, I recognise you from the club," I heard Boss say. "Have you seen the girl who was performing? Dark brown hair, slim, busty. She ran off, and I can't find her anywhere."

"Come to think of it, I think I have…" Lazarus replied. "I think she was on her way to the coffee shop down south."

"Yes, I've got her now!" Boss exclaimed in gratitude. "Thank you so much, drinks are on me whenever you come down to the club next."

"It's okay, glad I could help," Lazarus replied, letting out a forced chuckle.

I stayed in position, making sure I waited for a few minutes until I knew Boss was gone. I peered over the bin to see Lazarus making his way back to me. The coast was clear.

I got up and dusted myself off, still sweating profusely. Lazarus stared at me with his hazel eyes, and I had no idea what he was thinking right now. It was hard to read him. There was a long silence between us both.

"Thank you so much, I owe you my life," I said finally, swallowing.

I scratched my arm nervously. Lazarus seemed immersed in thought, his eyes not leaving mine for a second.

I could feel his eyes scan me from head to toe. Here I was, wearing such revealing clothes, and I felt massive waves of nervousness wash over me. He wouldn't say anything…he just kept staring at me.

But he seemed to stared at me out of what looked like genuine concern. Like he *wanted* to help me. He wasn't staring at me like I was a cheap whore. He was staring at me like I was a goddess.

It was a strange feeling I wasn't used to. I hadn't been expecting this at all. I thought he was just a man in the crowd who I would have forgotten after a few hours…but here he was, standing in front of me. Speaking to me. Staring at me.

And I didn't know what to think of that.

"I...erm..." I stumbled awkwardly, not knowing what to say. "I'll go home now," I managed finally.

"I won't let you go home alone at this time of night." He shrugged flatly. "There's a lot of creeps about. You don't want the same thing that happened inside to repeat itself, do you?"

"Of course not..." I mumbled, swallowing. This whole situation had caught me off-guard, and I could hardly think straight. I couldn't believe I was about to go home with this man.

But he'd *saved* me. And he didn't seem like he had sordid intentions. He hadn't laid a finger on me, and he'd helped me get away from a creep as well as my boss.

I knew for sure I wasn't going to make it a habit of going home with men I just met, but I also knew I didn't have much of an option. With Boss looking for me, I had to go somewhere he wouldn't think to look.

And I knew that he wouldn't think to look at Lazarus's place.

"I left my top and leggings in the club..." I murmured, dazed.

"It's fine, I can let you borrow one of my shirts. I've got some in my car." Lazarus shrugged.

"Thank you." I swallowed.

He gave me a reassuring smile before he turned on his heel and showed me to his car. My heart hammered against my chest as I followed him, not knowing how the night would unfold. Not knowing anything about this man...but the longer I spent with him, the more curious I was. He seemed like a mystery.

"Here, take my shirt," he said, as he slid into the driver's seat and ruffled through his belongings. He passed me the shirt as I slid into the passenger's seat, and I put it on. It smelt of his woody cologne, and I could feel sudden warmth overcome my body. I felt a sense of belonging.

"I don't think we can go back to my place...my boss might go there and he'll go nuts," I mumbled, as Lazarus began to drive.

"It's cool, you can come to my place."

"My sister is at home alone, I can't leave her there," I breathed, suddenly afraid.

"We'll pick her up first," Lazarus reassured me, pushing his foot down on the accelerator. "You have nothing to worry about."

I nodded sheepishly, feeling a little relieved. I didn't know if I were stupid to trust this man so quickly...but I guessed only time would tell as the night took its course. I would probably only stay at his place for a few nights until the heat died down with my boss, and then I would probably never see him again...

Right?

So why did the thought of never seeing this man again twist my insides into knots? A man who'd shown me genuine kindness and generosity...

Nobody had done that for me for a long time.

It was like he was my glimmer of hope. The small light in my shit life.

But I knew I couldn't get attached. He was just being kind to me...

Nothing more.

* * *

LAZARUS PARKED OUTSIDE of my apartment, and I swallowed in embarrassment, because he had to witness me living in such a rough area. An area where knife crime was paramount, and there were police patrolling the streets every other day. Not to mention my apartment was almost like living in a bin.

I shook my head, doing my best to push my doubts and insecurities to the back of my mind. I made my way inside my apartment, and he followed suit, not saying a word. I was welcomed by Sophia, still sitting on the couch, and she was still watching *Prison Break*. She'd probably gotten through about three episodes since I'd been away.

"You're still awake? I thought I told you not to stay up too long," I commented, smiling.

"You know I can't keep my promises." Sophia giggled, turning around to face me. "I was enjoying the show too much. I only have two seasons left."

I nodded in response, but I knew we couldn't stick around here for long and just spend time talking. We needed to get out of here, fast.

"Anyway, we need to leave here now, in case my boss shows up." I sighed, exhausted. "I got into a bit of a sticky situation at work."

Sophia got up on her feet with an alarmed expression on her face.

"What did you do?" she asked. Her eyes darted backwards and forwards between me and Lazarus, looking confused as to why he was here.

"It doesn't matter, just get a few of your things, and let's go," I said quickly.

"And who's this sexy man?" she said coyly, biting her finger at Lazarus.

I wanted to snap at her for being inappropriate, but Lazarus let out an amused chuckle.

"He's a friend from work," I lied, smiling.

Sophia nodded.

"Okay, I'll go and get my things," she exclaimed.

"Make sure you get all your things!" Lazarus called out after her, as she left the living room.

"What do you mean, all of our things?" I mumbled, turning around to face him.

"You won't be living here anymore. You're coming with me," Lazarus said, his eyes piercing mine.

"W-What?" I swallowed. I was caught off guard by this, and didn't know how to react. "But after today, I won't have a job, I'll hardly have any money..."

"Don't worry about any of that," Lazarus reassured me.

"B-But..."

"Just trust me," Lazarus soothed. "We can talk about this later."

I had no idea what to think of this, and I had no idea what any of this meant. But I also knew I had to trust him...

So I let out a feeble nod.

"Erm, okay..." I managed, scratching my arm awkwardly.

* * *

AFTER WE GOT all of our clothes, we left the flat and drove off with Lazarus. Lazarus made his way to his apartment, driving down the motorway at high speed. He played songs on his Aux to try and lighten the mood and put us at ease, from songs by The Weeknd to songs by French Montana. I tried to relax, but my heart was hammering against my chest the entire journey.

He arrived at his apartment, parking his car in the drive-way, and we made our way inside.

He had a beautiful penthouse apartment, with a gorgeous city skyline view of London through the windows. It looked so expensive...

I'd never seen anything like it before. Something so magnificent, so breathtaking. Working-class people like me never got luxuries like this. I knew there was more to this man from the first time I laid eyes on him. I knew he looked powerful and wealthy.

Why the hell was he helping somebody like *me*?

"Wow, your house is beautiful…" I murmured, and Sophia clapped her hands in delight, unable to believe her eyes.

"Thank you," Lazarus replied, chuckling appreciatively.

"Is it all right if I go to bed now?" Sophia asked. "I'm shattered."

"Yeah, just take your stuff up to the spare bedroom, first on the left," Lazarus explained.

"Thank you," Sophia said gratefully.

Before I knew it, me and Lazarus were alone. I swallowed a lump in my throat, feeling my eyes well with tears. Being in this apartment just reminded me of a life I could never have.

A life I could only dream of living.

After all, women like me were never destined for anything good in life…*right?*

"Come and sit down." Lazarus smiled, beckoning me towards the sofa.

I nodded, and sat down next to him.

"Thank you for all this." I swallowed, and then thought I might as well ask, because the curiosity was killing me. "Ahm…why are you helping me?"

Lazarus let out a deep sigh.

"You looked like you were in trouble. I saw you running out of the club," he admitted.

"Yeah, the client was being really sexual and tried to sleep with me. I had to find a way out of there," I muttered, not wanting to remember the shit-show that happened earlier. "When Boss finds me, he's going to kill me."

"He won't find you here. I'm sorry for the way you've been treated at the club," Lazarus sighed. He paused. "But what is a girl like you even doing working there? You didn't look like you fit in at all. You looked like an outsider...like you hated it."

"Trust me, I don't want to," I exhaled. "I don't have a choice."

"Why not?"

"I work at a coffee shop in the daytime, but the money isn't enough for me to pay all the bills. I have the responsibility to take care of my little sister too. She relies on me." I shook my head. "I tried so hard to find another job to do at night...but I had no luck. So I started at that club, out of desperation."

Lazarus folded his arms uneasily, furrowing his eyebrows in concern.

"I hate it so much. I hate having to get naked and stripping myself of my dignity. I hate that dirty men think me doing this job is equivalent to me giving consent for them to touch me sexually, when it isn't." I rattled my fists, suddenly seething. Needing to vent. Needing to let out my frustration and hurt, because I'd never had anyone to speak to about how I felt before, and this man seemed willing to listen, whether or not he cared. "And the worst thing is, my boss keeps most of the money I make there. I tried to leave so many times, but my boss wouldn't let me. He would come to my house and force me to come back. He said that without me, there would be no business or clients. I tried not to go... but he started hitting me."

"That bastard laid his hands on you?" Lazarus seethed, his blood boiling, murder written all over his face.

His veins pulsated their way to the surface of his skin, but he grabbed hold of his wrist, doing his best to calm down for my sake. He probably didn't want to scare me. He wanted to *protect* me...

"I wish I'd come there sooner..." he trailed off.

"It's okay, you weren't to know," I whispered. "You didn't

even know who I was before tonight." My eyes found his, and my eyes brimmed with tears. "I don't want to burden you with my problems. I'm so sorry. You didn't have to do all of this."

"I want to help you," Lazarus breathed. "I don't want you working at that place again. I can get you a job elsewhere. You can stay here until you find a new place to stay in."

And there it was again. His gorgeous pale eyes staring at me. I was getting distracted, but it was hard for me to stay focused around this man. I felt goosebumps, and my heart beat faster.

He was so beautiful, with a broad, muscular build, and a face that looked like it had been carved by Greek gods.

And he was staring at me.

As if he *cared* about me.

Nobody had ever cared about me before...

"Hey..." Lazarus said suddenly, causing me to snap out of my thoughts. His eyes darted from my face to my body, and fell, as if he'd just seen a ghost.

As if somebody had just walked over his grave.

What was wrong with him? What had I done wrong?

"What are all those scars on your chest?" he asked.

I gasped, dismayed. Dismayed because the realization hit me that he'd seen my scars...

I clutched the area where my scars were, doing my best to hide them, even though the damage was already done. It was no use.

And now he'd pointed them out, I was reminded of all of my painful memories. The stories behind the scars, which I tried so hard to forget. Tried so hard to bury beneath the surface. Tried so hard to move on from.

"Who did this to you?" Lazarus demanded angrily, seething. "If it was your boss, I swear to God..."

"No, it wasn't my boss!" I cried out, and before I knew it, I broke down into sobs. Rocking myself backwards and forwards as every terrible thing replayed itself over and over in my head, repetitively, like a form of torture.

I couldn't breathe.

I couldn't fucking breathe.

"These are scars from my past..."

I trailed off my sentence, my chest heaving as blood continued to roar throughout my body.

"It all started eighteen years ago..."

BOSS

I made my way into the coffee shop where the man I'd met outside the club told me to go. I rubbed my chin in thought as I immersed myself in my surroundings, trying to locate her and pinpoint where she was.

"Weird, I can't see her anywhere," I murmured to myself.

I noticed the manager collecting some cash from the till, so I looked up and beckoned him.

"Hey, have you seen a pretty brunette girl in the shop in the past hour?" I called out.

"Nope, not had one brunette girl walk in since the morning. Sorry," he replied flatly.

I shook my fists angrily, suddenly seething.

That guy *lied* to me.

He was probably her boyfriend.

I would make sure he paid for this.

Paid for wasting my damn motherfucking time.

RAVEN

*M*y heart pounded against my chest, and heat roared in my ears as I slowly allowed my walls to break down as I spoke to Lazarus about my past. I knew me and him were practically strangers, and I was trusting him far too quickly, but what other choice did I have? I had to stay with him or I would be subject to abuse from my boss.

And I knew which option I would rather choose.

Lazarus listened to me without judgement. He didn't make me feel stupid for feeling the way I did. He was understanding and caring, so I found myself becoming more comfortable around him. I had a brutal, terrifying past which I hated being reminded of.

But talking about things always helped to ease the weight off your shoulders...

"My parents used to hurt and hit me a lot. I'd never done anything wrong. My adopted sister Sophia used to be up in her room, listening to the noise," I began, breathing heavily.

* * *

I SOBBED as Mum slapped me across the face, and Dad screamed bloody murder angrily, letting out one blood-curdling scream after the other.

I was terrified.

I could feel tears slide down my cheeks, pit-pattering on the ground in tiny little droplets.

Drip.

Drop.

Drip.

Drop.

"Go to your room and stay there. No food for two days," Mum snarled.

I let out a deep breath, my lungs constricting for air. I felt like I was suffocating, and I couldn't breathe.

I shakily made my way out of the room, my whole body trembling. I stopped at the door, doing my best to recollect myself and calm down before I had a panic attack.

And that was when I heard Mum say the next words to Dad.

"I'll see you upstairs in bed, babe." She smiled before pulling him in for a kiss.

If only she knew...

If only she really knew what my father was like, then she wouldn't be so loving towards him...

* * *

I LAY IN BED, still trembling. Staring at the ceiling, doing my best to count sheep and drift off to sleep before the monster would come into my room.

I couldn't let him come in here.

I couldn't...

"I'm sorry your mum snapped at you, babe," a deep, low voice said quietly. I jolted up.

This couldn't be happening...

The monster was here.

"Now," Dad said, leaning over my bed. "A man has needs from his beautiful daughter."

I screamed as tears fought their way down my cheeks.

It felt like I was trapped.

Trapped in an endless cycle of pain with no way out.

I couldn't bear it anymore.

I couldn't bear it...

When was I ever going to escape this nightmare?

* * *

"My dad would come into my room and rape me." I wept, feeling my head sear with the painful memories.

Reliving every terrible nightmare.

"The day I couldn't take it anymore, I tried to talk to my mum about it…" I murmured hollowly. "She called me a lunatic and beat the daylights out of me for accusing her husband of doing such a thing. She left me and my sister locked in a shed for weeks." I let my hair drape down to hide my face.

"One day, she left it unlocked, and that's when I ran away with my sister. We ran as far away as possible from the city, we didn't care where the trains took us. We just wanted to get away." I swallowed hard.

"We were dirty and hungry. One day we sat down begging for change on the streets. A man gave us a strange look, so we quickly made to run, thinking he was going to contact social services." I peeked out at him through my hair.

"He ran after us, and said he didn't mean any harm. He said he wanted to help us and take us to a shelter that caters to the homeless, where we would have food to eat and a mattress to sleep on." A small smile appeared on my face.

"We were happy the man wanted to help us, and we

agreed. We went with him and he took us to his house. This was confusing because we thought he was taking us to a homeless shelter." I sunk back behind my hair.

"A man came to the doorstep and took my sister away from me. He took her to the homeless shelter just like we agreed. They told me to wait at the house, because there wasn't enough room for one more in the car, and said they'd take me to the homeless shelter next. I was thrilled, thinking that finally me and my sister were going to escape from our nightmare parents." I wiped my eyes.

"When the man came back, he didn't take me to the homeless shelter. The truth is, he'd only taken her because she was the younger one out of us both and he said that I was old enough to 'go into work.'"

I broke off, shivering. Shivering as I recounted the full extent of what *going into work* meant. Lazarus stared at me with sorrow.

Like he was reliving my nightmares with me.

"He forced me to become a drug mule, and I was sexually assaulted by the men in the house." I trembled shakily. "I was only a teenager. I was terrified." I sniffed.

"They forced me to swallow drugs and then cough them out at a different place. I was lucky I didn't die. One day, they left the car door open while they were collecting a drug shipment. I sought this opportunity to escape and ran away. I collected my sister from the shelter, and the woman in charge told us she would offer us a lift to wherever we needed to go, it was the least she could do. I asked her to send us to London. We were thrown into the care system, and then let out as soon as we turned sixteen. I was the first one to get out." I huddled into the corner of my seat.

"This was when I got my own place and started working at a coffee shop to make a living. But the coffee shop didn't bring me enough money, and soon, I started working at the strip club." I peeked at Lazarus again.

"When my sister left the care system at sixteen, she moved in with me. I told her that I work at a pub, because I was so ashamed of how I was making my living…and now this is where I am today."

I found myself taking deep breaths in and out, my chest heaving before I broke into fresh sobs, and I couldn't hold them back. Lazarus took my hand into his, squeezing it, trying to give me the reassurance that it was okay, and he was here for me. That the past remained in the past, even though my demons kept battling with me in my mind.

I guessed we all had skeletons in the closet.

"I wish that things didn't have to be like this," I murmured. "For years, I've been praying that this will all come to an end. To this day, I still don't know why I haven't taken my own life. It gets so hard for me sometimes, and I feel weak. Like nothing will make me feel better. I feel like I have nothing left to live for. Like I'm trapped in an endless spiral that I can't get out of."

"I'm so sorry that this happened to you," Lazarus breathed, cupping my face in his hands, drying my tears with his thumbs. "I'll do everything within my power to help you." He broke off, letting out a deep sigh.

"You have everything to live for. I'm here for you now. You're strong, and you've made it this far. I know it can sometimes feel like the world's against you, and that everything that happens to you is bad…but it's your past that shapes you into a stronger individual. Everything happens for a reason. Suicide isn't the answer, baby. You're loved. What would your sister do if you left her all alone to fend for herself? She'd be heartbroken."

I could feel my eyes glimmer with tears, because deep down I knew he was right.

"I'm going to make sure you don't live another day in your life without a smile on your face. I'll protect you with my dying breath."

Before I knew it, the room went eerily quiet. Neither of us said a word, but his eyes continued to burn into mine.

And then Lazarus brought his mouth down onto mine.

I didn't know if I was rushing things. Here I was, kissing a man I'd just met.

But he made me feel safe.

He made me feel complete.

He made me feel like I could trust him.

I'd never spoken to anybody about my past.

But in the moment...I didn't care if I was rushing things. I just wanted to enjoy his embrace.

I felt at home.

He was my knight in shining armor.

He just saved me from a life of slaving away at a strip club.

BOSS

I entered Raven's apartment, hoping she was here.

"Doesn't sound like there's anyone at home..." I murmured to myself.

I rolled my eyes sarcastically before making my way deeper inside her apartment. She must be in her bedroom sleeping, or something.

I entered her bedroom to see the wardrobe doors wide open, and hangers tossed about on the floor. There were no clothes remaining.

I darted my eyes to her bed, which was also empty.

Panic-stricken, I bolted out of the room, heading to her sister Sophia's room.

Only to be greeted by the very same things...

I found myself screaming bloody murder, unable to believe my eyes. What the fuck was going on?

"All of her clothes are gone! Where has she fucking ran off to?" I bellowed.

I could feel my blood rush to my cheeks as my whole body set on fire with anger.

I was in a state of rage. Nobody crossed me and got away with it.

Nobody.

"This isn't over, Raven Emmerdale!" I roared.

RAVEN

*M*e and Lazarus got intimate pretty fast. Everything was going perfectly.

He took me and my sister to parties. We took long night strolls talking about our plans for the future. He worked in an office, and he had a great income.

My sister was happy at last. *I* was happy.

He treated me so well. He bought me things I wanted, he took me to fancy restaurants, he admired my body and respected and loved me.

I was already so attached. He was already so important to me.

I loved him, and he loved me. He was my hero. My saving grace.

I never thought I was going to get my lucky break, and here it was.

I was content.

Then why, *why* did I have to stick my nose into something I shouldn't have and ruin everything?

Why did I follow him that night?

Why didn't I just stay at home and mind my own business?

You see, Lazarus was my first love. He made me feel special, he made me feel wanted. He didn't treat me like I was worthless.

But happily ever afters didn't exist in my world. I was a woman who carried so much baggage, and had so many skeletons in the closet. So many demons from my past haunting my mind.

I should have known better than to put my trust in a man I hardly knew. He may have been sweet on the surface, but the fact of the matter was that I didn't really know him at all. He knew so much about me, but it seemed like he was just putting up a façade. Putting up a sweet exterior, when really, he was battling demons of his own.

Meeting Lazarus turned my life upside down, and not in a good way. Because the more time went on, the more the cracks on the surface began to appear. There were so many things that I learnt about him which I never would have expected. I was too blinded by love to realise what was staring me right in the face. The red flags had been waving around me, but I ignored them, so desperate was I for my own happily ever after.

Everything I went through with him 'happened for a reason,' just like he'd told me when he took me to his penthouse.

I've told you the story of how I met Lazarus.

Now I'm going to tell you the story of how Lazarus turned my life upside down.

* * *

"LAZARUS HASN'T COME HOME today. Why would he be out so late if he worked in an office?" I murmured to myself, pacing around my bedroom. "Maybe he's gone to see a friend. Maybe I'm overreacting."

I rubbed my chin in thought, furrowing my eyebrows.

"But he hasn't even texted or called me, telling me not to wait up for him. He hasn't replied to any of my messages." I broke off, shaking my head. "I think I should go and look for him."

I stared at my wardrobe, and a small smile formed on my lips, a blush creeping to my cheeks.

"I should dress sexy and surprise him," I murmured to myself, and giggled with anticipation.

I walked over to my wardrobe, and slid into a tight bodycon sparkly red mini-dress, paired with red high heels. I plaited my hair and put on some red lipgloss. I hoped Lazarus would like my look and my outfit.

And then I turned on my heel, and headed out of Lazarus's penthouse.

I knew I had nothing to fear with my old boss anymore if I went out, because I now had Lazarus's protection. He said he would protect me with his dying breath…

So I knew I had nothing to worry about.

RAVEN

$\mathcal{I}$ made my way down the motorway in one of Lazarus's cars, driving at a high speed, accelerating further with every passing second.

"This traffic is a nightmare," I muttered.

"Why have you dragged me into this again?" Sophia replied beside me.

"Well, I'm following Lazarus," I remarked, rolling my eyes.

Sophia sighed heavily, appearing agitated with me, like this was the worst idea in the world.

"Just concentrate on the road!" she snapped.

I rolled my eyes again as I continued to drive. I'd managed to trace Lazarus's location through my phone, because he'd left the app on. I hoped he was all right, and he wasn't in any trouble. I was worried about him, so I thought it would only be right to check on him. I was sure he wouldn't mind.

* * *

THE NIGHT WAS PITCH BLACK, the stars dimly lighting the sky. I'd reached the location my phone told me Lazarus was currently. I parked outside a few streets down, so my car wouldn't be in plain sight, and I wouldn't get caught.

Me and Sophia cautiously made our way to the house. It had big oak trees, and was beautifully refurbished. It was a huge mansion, and I found it hard to believe my eyes.

I cautiously opened the gate and made my way down the driveway, Sophia following closely behind me. Suddenly, I heard voices in the back garden.

It sounded like Lazarus's voice, in a heated conversation with a few other men.

I tiptoed to the garden, making sure not to make a sound. Me and Sophia hid behind a bin, crouching downwards so that we wouldn't bait ourselves.

I furrowed my eyebrows in confusion, as I watched the scene play out in front of me. I couldn't believe my eyes.

Lazarus was wearing a cop outfit, and he was standing between two men. One of the men was dark-skinned with dreadlocks, and was wearing tracksuit bottoms. The other was white, his blond hair tied in a manbun, with a rugged beard, and scars all over his face and body. His white t-shirt was soaked with blood, and I had no idea why.

"Have you disposed of the body?" Lazarus hissed.

"Yes, Boss," said the blond man, dusting himself off.

"Okay, good," Lazarus confirmed. "Both of you need to get out of here as soon as possible. I'll deal with the rest, and clean up your mess. Make sure you burn that t-shirt, and anything else that connects you to the murder. I'll handle things down at the police station."

The men nodded, as if they were his lapdogs and did everything Lazarus told them to do.

"He's a police officer?" I whispered to myself, even more

confused than I had been earlier. "Why would he lie to me and tell me that he works in an office?"

I found this whole situation so strange, I couldn't make sense of any of it. Those men had taken care of a body, and instead of arresting them, Lazarus was telling them he would take care of things from his side?

I could feel my heart pound against my chest as I began sweating profusely. The full extent of what was happening suddenly hit me from a million different directions at once, like daggers straight to my heart.

But I didn't want to believe what my mind was telling me. I wanted to carry on following him to put my mind at rest, because this whole thing could just be a huge misunderstanding on my part. I wanted to think the best of Lazarus, not believe he was capable of doing something so sordid, not after everything he had done for me...

There must have been a logical explanation behind all of this. Maybe he was an undercover cop, so he wasn't allowed to tell me his job as part of his role...?

"We better get out of here before he sees us," Sophia hissed in my ear, causing me to jolt out of my thoughts.

I nodded timidly, feeling my throat go dry, hardly able to compose a sentence because it was like I'd suddenly forgotten how to speak.

Before I knew it, Lazarus had turned around and he was making his way inside the mansion, while the other two men turned in the opposite direction, headed to their car. I grabbed hold of Sophia, pushing her closer to the bin so we were hidden properly as the men exited the back garden. I blew a sigh of relief as I heard the revving of the engine, and watched them drive away. We hadn't been made.

"Let's get out of here, please," Sophia said shakily. "I'm scared, Raven."

"Not yet," I murmured, because I was in a state of confusion, and I needed answers. I got to my feet, helping her up too. I needed to follow Lazarus inside of the mansion to see what he was doing. I needed to put my mind at ease. I couldn't just go home with Sophia and act like nothing had happened. Everything I'd seen would plague my thoughts all night long and straight into the day.

Lazarus had made his way to the basement of the mansion, and he was in a heated conversation with two new men. One looked Polish, and the other one looked Russian. They were smoking cigarettes, taking in Lazarus's words to the last detail.

Me and Sophia hid behind a wall so that could listen to their conversation.

"Is our shipment ready to collect yet?" Lazarus asked, folding his arms.

"We've been told it's arriving tomorrow, Boss," said the Russian, shrugging.

"When and where?" Lazarus snarled.

"Four in the afternoon, at the docks," the Polish man stated.

Lazarus nodded in approval. "Now we've got our shipments back on track we're finally back in the game. The Manzellas ruling the fucking streets. I'm gonna be the biggest goddamn drug dealer in London. The Surenos won't know what hit them. We're taking over their territory, along with the Mexican motherfuckers, and the Italians." Lazarus chuckled. "Our cartel will rule the fucking country...because I'm the kingpin. Everybody will fear me."

"You're gonna rule, Boss," the Polish man exclaimed. "We're gonna move so much product, and if anyone tries to cross us it means war."

I could feel the colour drain right out of my face as I went stone-white in shock, unable to believe my ears.

The Manzellas...

The two words that came out of Lazarus's mouth replayed themselves over and over, like a form of mother-fucking torture.

I couldn't breathe.

I couldn't fucking breathe.

Lazarus was the kingpin of the Mafia whose members assaulted me and took my sister away from me?

I didn't want to believe what I was hearing...but I'd heard it come straight from his mouth. I couldn't turn a blind eye to that fact and act like nothing had happened.

This must have meant he was a dirty cop...this whole cop façade was just a front to cover up his tracks.

I couldn't believe he'd been hiding something so big from me this whole time. I couldn't believe he lied to me. I thought he loved me.

Why did everyone I got close to always have to break my heart?

I thought he was different. He was one of them this whole time.

I could never trust anybody again...

I found tears welling in my eyes, and they fell uncontrol-lably, I was unable to hold them back. I broke into sobs, my whole body shaking into a frenzy. I couldn't comprehend this situation. I prayed it was just a nightmare, and I would wake up...

I fucking prayed...

"Raven, we need to get out of here before they see us!" Sophia whispered desperately. "Come on, this isn't the time or the place to start crying!"

A sudden deep voice caused me to jolt upwards, and my heart leapt to my throat. I watched my life flash before my eyes.

"Guys, did you hear that sound?" came Lazarus's voice.

"Yeah, sounded like someone crying," the Polish man remarked.

We'd been made.

I was suddenly terrified. After everything I'd just learnt about Lazarus, I had no idea what he was capable of, or what he would do. He'd gone from a sweet office man to a mafia kingpin within seconds...

My heart pounded against my chest as my tear-filled eyes slowly made their way upwards from the ground, with Sophia shivering behind me, and I saw Lazarus looming over me, his shadow dominating the room.

Bloody murder written all over his face.

"What the fuck are you two doing here?" Lazarus sneered, his voice dropping to barely above a whisper.

Echoing across the room.

RAVEN

"*R*aven got worried about you because it was so late and you still hadn't come home..." Sophia trembled, doing her best to explain herself on my behalf, and rectify the situation.

But I knew it was no use.

Nothing was going to save me from facing the music.

"So you fucking followed me, you psychotic bitch?" Lazarus snarled, his eyes burning into mine, as if he were staring right into my soul.

His eyes were filled with darkness, appearing hollow, void, completely empty of emotion.

He no longer stared at me like I was a work of art. Like I was the most beautiful woman in the world. Like he admired me and respected me. The way he would worship my body, and make me feel like a goddess whenever we slept together, despite all of my scars and marks...

There was no love left.

He looked so angry, it looked like he wanted to kill.

And it terrified me.

It fucking terrified me.

"Dressed like that at this time of night, with all the creepy men about?" Lazarus snarled, cocking his head to the side. Disgust was written all over his face as he looked at my bare skin. *"Giving them ideas?"*

"No, I dressed like this for you!" I pleaded, sobbing. "I wanted to look nice to see you!"

Lazarus rolled his eyes, not caring what I had to say. I didn't know what I could say or do to fix this.

There was no fixing this...

"It's not okay to fucking follow me around and interfere in my private business!" Lazarus barked in a low voice that caused my skin to burn as I quivered underneath his gaze. "I barely met you a few weeks ago, and this is how you behave! Now you've heard everything and you're a goddamn liability!" He broke off, seething, rattling his fists angrily.

"Why are you shouting at me like I'm in the wrong?" I snapped back. "You run the drug cartel whose members harassed me all those years ago! Who took my sister away from me! I poured my heart out to you, and you acted oblivious the whole time. The whole time, you were part of the criminal organization..."

"Go take the sorry act somewhere else, you're just a pathetic little stripper," Lazarus snarled, not caring whether he was hurting my feelings. Not caring about the pain and anguish he put me in making me relive my torture from all those years ago. He knew just how to push my buttons, just how to make me feel like I was worth nothing. Bringing my background and my career into the situation, even though he knew I didn't have a choice when I was living that way... "When you wear clothes like that and dance in front of old men, how can you not expect them to do those things to you?"

I jolted backwards, mortified. I felt humiliated, and now, I couldn't stop the tears from falling. I may have been a stripper, but there was no justification for rape. Rape was *never* the victim's fault, I knew that, and I had to keep reminding myself of that no matter what...

"You just crossed the line, Lazarus," I croaked. "A man's dirty mind has nothing to do with what a girl wears."

Lazarus rolled his eyes, as if he really couldn't care less about my opinion. And that stung me more than I could ever imagine. It felt like somebody had torn my heart out of my chest, and was hammering at it with a chainsaw.

I loved this man...

It had only been a few weeks, but I genuinely *loved* him...

"Raven, you're a stripper?" Sophia spat bitterly, jolting me out of my thoughts. I turned around to face her, and this only triggered my tears even more. I could see the hurt written all over her face, because she hadn't known about what I did to make money. I felt even guiltier that I hadn't told the truth, and she had to hear it from somebody else before she heard it from me. "You told me you work in a pub! How could you lie to your own sister?"

"I'm sorry, babe..." I breathed, my chest heaving. "I didn't want you to know, because I wanted to protect you. You're too innocent for my world."

Sophia opened her mouth to speak, but then closed it, as if she were trying to stop herself from saying something she would regret. She shook her head, taking it into her hands, and rocking herself back and forth.

She looked back up at me, her eyes welling with tears. "I understand, but the fact you couldn't trust me enough to tell me shows what I really mean to you," she whispered shakily.

"Sophia, don't say that..." I pleaded, not wanting to fall out with my sister. She was all I had. I couldn't bear hurting her. I couldn't bear the fact she was upset and angry with me...

Before I could justify myself, Sophia turned on her heel,

making her way out of the basement, her eyes fixated on the floor the whole time.

Lazarus let out a low laugh beside me, the corners of his mouth forming into a smirk as he watched the scene play out. He was amused. Amused by my pain, the fucking bastard...

"You manage to make everyone leave you, don't you?" he sneered.

I balled my hands into fists, hardly able to hide my rage. I was so angry. So, so fucking angry.

"Why are you behaving like this?" I shouted. "I didn't do anything wrong. I just wanted to check up on you, and you're talking to me like I'm some sort of animal..." I trailed off as tears threatened to spill down my cheeks again. My heart felt like it was about to explode.

Just when I thought my life was getting better, leaving the strip club, living with a man who took care of me, provided for me...

It felt like everything was slipping through my hands like water.

Like it had just been a dream, and none of it had actually happened.

My past yet again coming back to bite me in the ass.

"Raven, I can't be arsed with this shit right now," Lazarus spat, rolling his eyes agitatedly. "I've got stuff on my fucking plate that I need to take care of. More important than your fucking emotional episodes. Grow a fucking backbone and go home. We'll talk about this later."

I balled my hands into fists again as Lazarus continued to invalidate my emotions. Dismissing me like I meant nothing to him.

"You've got another thing coming if you think I'm gonna talk to you after the way you just spoke to me," I snapped back.

Before he had the chance to respond, I turned on my heel, and began trudging out of the basement, my surroundings blurred around me as I struggled to stay focused on the here and now.

Not wanting to believe that Lazarus was a bad man.

Not wanting my fairytale to end so abruptly.

But deep down…I knew it was over.

And now, I didn't know what I was going to do.

LAZARUS

I sighed to myself as I watched Raven walk away. She'd wasted enough of my damn time with her temper tantrum, when I could have been speaking to my men about how we were going to grow and make money. I was pissed off to say the fucking least. The woman knew how to get on my last fucking nerve.

"Women are something else, man, Jesus Christ." Luis laughed from beside me, amused.

The last thing I needed was my men fucking jesting me.

"Where did you even find such a psychopath, Boss?" said Tariq, joining in on the laughter. "Weird, you never told us you have a girlfriend."

I rolled my eyes angrily, shaking my head. Feeling my anger boil to the point my head was searing in pain from my fucking temper.

"That's because she's not my girlfriend," I snarled, wanting to put an end to this mockery. After the way Raven had just humiliated me in front of my men…she was going to have to pay.

Tariq and Luis's eyes pierced mine with intrigue and

curiosity, wanting to know who the hell Raven was if she wasn't my girlfriend, even though she believed herself to be.

"I went to a strip club one night because I hadn't been laid in ages," I muttered. "I saw her up on the podium performing. She was sexy, I gotta admit. She caught my eye. I was having drinks, and I saw her boss bothering her and forcing her to dance with some creep.

"Later, I saw her running out of the bar. I followed her and told her I'd help her out. The dumb bitch believed everything, she was such an easy lay. It's nice knowing that she's not sleeping with other guys, while I fuck about all I want. I have a woman who feeds off my attention, a woman who's willing to be my fucking lapdog. Hanging off my every word." I shrugged my shoulders.

"It's not her that's making me keep her around. It's the fact that I feed off of her weakness. I feed off her vulnerability. I know I can treat her however I want, and she won't leave. Because she knows that if she leaves me, she's got nothing going for herself. If she leaves me, she's back living on the bare minimum, dancing on a pole for disgusting men so she can get by." I folded my arms.

"And I tell you, none of the shit she just heard here will fucking matter. She won't have it in her to leave. She'll turn a blind eye to it, give me chance after chance, no matter what I throw at her, no matter what she finds out. She'll cry like a bitch, wallow in self-pity. But the bitch loves me. She has nowhere else to go. She's so stupid…as if I'd have feelings for a fucking stripper."

I could feel the corners of my mouth form into a smirk. I hadn't had this feeling for a long time. The feeling of a woman being completely at my submission. Completely at my mercy.

I fucking loved it.

Tariq and Luis found this just as amusing as I did. They

roared with appreciative laughter beside me, hanging off my every word. Even they were my fucking lapdogs. They knew if they so much as looked at me the wrong way, I'd put a bullet through their fucking brains.

"Boss, that's cold, man. But I rate you. With all that lying, you got to bed one hot chick." Luis laughed.

"Well, I ain't got time to do the whole commitment thing with women," I snarled. "I've gotta focus on business and pushing product...expanding territory. Making money, getting more power, taking out rival cartels. Competing on the fucking streets." I broke off. "Not women. A real man doesn't have the time for fucking distractions."

They nodded to me in approval. I took my box of cigarettes out of my pocket, putting one into my mouth, and then set it alight, allowing the smoke to cloud my lungs.

Needing to clear my head and relax.

RAVEN

$\mathcal{I}$ sat in bed rubbing my eyes, staring at the ceiling as what happened today replayed itself over and over in my head, like a form of motherfucking torture.

I'd never seen this side of Lazarus before. He was always so sweet and kind to me. I don't know what got into him.

The more I thought about it, the more I hounded myself with the different possibilities and outcomes that could have happened.

Maybe I went too far by following him.

Maybe I should have just minded my own business.

If I hadn't followed him, maybe he would have stayed the sweet and charming man he was, and nothing would have been ruined between us. What I didn't know couldn't hurt me, right?

But it was too late now. I couldn't undo it, and I had to deal with the aftermath.

But I didn't expect him to be so misogynistic.

His opinion about strippers was wrong. There was no shame in being a stripper. At the end of the day, a job was a job, and everybody was just trying to put food on the table.

Who had the right to knock another person's hustle? Why should females be punished for a male's dirty mind?

Maybe he just got angry in the heat of the moment. I didn't want to believe Lazarus was a bad man. I wanted to see the best in him, even after everything I'd just found out.

After all, I did just find out he was a drug cartel kingpin, and not somebody who worked in an office.

I didn't know what to do. Well and truly, I felt fucking stuck. I was damned if I do, *damned if I don't.*

Maybe if I forgave Lazarus, we could move past this. Act like it never happened. Go back to normal.

I just didn't want to go back to the life I had before I knew him...

He gave me that small, small glimmer of hope. Like he was my light at the end of the tunnel.

So I deliberately wanted to act oblivious to what was staring at me right in the face. *Even if it killed me.*

The sound of a voice caused me to jolt, and snap out of my thoughts. I did my best to compose myself and get myself together, pushing my harrowing thoughts to the back of my mind.

Wanting and needing to forget.

Lazarus was standing in front of me in just his boxers. He had a woeful expression on his face, like he was hurt and upset.

Just as upset as I was.

"Hey babe?" he breathed timidly.

I got up on my feet, shaking. Letting out a sigh as I regained my composure.

"What?" I asked.

"I'm sorry for the way I spoke to you earlier," he sighed. "I was out of line. I didn't mean what I said." He trailed off, letting out a deep exhalation. "You're beautiful, and it isn't your fault for what those men did to you. I just got angry because you'd found out about the cartel. I wanted to keep you away from it because I didn't want to put you in danger, babe. It was better that you didn't know..."

I could feel tears well in my eyes, but I bit my lip in an attempt to stop them spilling. I didn't know if he was apologizing for the sake of it, or because he genuinely wanted to fix things between us...

But either way, I wanted to believe the latter. I wanted to believe what my heart wanted me to believe, even though my mind was screaming at me to believe different.

I wanted my own happily ever after. I didn't want to see his flaws.

"And as for those members from all those years ago, I wasn't in the Mafia business back then," Lazarus explained. "So I wouldn't have known who they even were, let alone have known about what they did to you. I'm sorry, babe. Do you forgive me?"

I found myself rubbing my chin, immersed in my own thoughts.

What he said was wrong, but how could I not forgive the man who saved me from my boss?

How could I not forgive the man who made my heart skip a beat every time he looked at me?

How could I not forgive the man who was providing for me and Sophia?

I gave him a nod, and a smile formed on his lips.

"We all make mistakes, babe..." I reassured him. "As long as it doesn't happen again."

I let out a sigh I didn't know I was holding.

"And no more secrets," I said, folding my arms.

"No more secrets," Lazarus confirmed, his eyes piercing mine.

"Now come here, babe. I missed you." I giggled as I watched him step closer, his eyes darkening with desire.

Even though I knew he was lying through his teeth.

"You don't have to tell me twice, baby girl," he growled, and then crashed his mouth down on mine, kissing me with such an urgency that it was hard to breathe. He was rough, passionate, and needy. He tore my clothes off, throwing me backwards onto the bed so my ass was in the air, and slapped my ass so hard I whimpered, biting down on the pillow to stop myself from screaming.

He slapped my ass again, one time, two times, three times...

Then he began rubbing it to soothe it, and lowered his body down onto mine, cupping my breasts from behind and leaving a trail of soft, wet kisses on my back that caused me to quiver and moan uncontrollably underneath his touch.

"So sexy..." he groaned, flipping me around and taking my nipples into his mouth. "So fucking sexy..."

I whimpered in pleasure, allowing him to continue having his way with me.

Not knowing what I was signing myself up for.

Not knowing that the worst was yet to come.

I'd survived a little argument...

But was I really ready to survive a war?

RAVEN

"*B*ill, come tidy up the shop once you're done in the kitchen!" Lucy called out as she sorted through the change in the till.

I was at my daytime shift at the coffee shop. Even though I'd been living with Lazarus, I didn't want to leave this job, because Lucy was a great friend to me here, and I didn't want to feel lonely. I wanted to make some money for myself too, so I didn't feel like I was sponging off another man.

Lucy was a gorgeous woman, with creamy skin, big blue eyes, bright red hair, and we'd been friends for years. She was kind, funny, and caring, and was one of the few people who made my life bearable.

"Babe, I'm so happy to see you so smiley all the time," she exclaimed, causing me to snap out of my thoughts. I smiled back at her, a blush creeping on my cheeks. Me and Lazarus had been good as ever for a while now, it was like I'd never found out about those things that day. I preferred it like this, with the bad stuff out of sight, out of mind. We could just focus on each other.

Being crazy in love.

"Thanks, babe." I giggled.

"He must really be something, huh?" Lucy grinned. "You haven't been able to wipe that smile off your face for weeks."

I laughed, unable to stop blushing as I thought about Lazarus and the last few weeks we'd spent together. In bed, on dates...

"I love him, Lucy." The words rolled out of my mouth.

"I know you do, babe." Lucy giggled. "Just know that if he ever breaks your heart, he'll have me to answer to." She pointed her fingers up pretentiously.

I smiled.

"Man, I haven't been out in so long," I admitted. "Ever since I left the strip club, I've been in bed every night bingeing Netflix. I need a girls' night out."

"I know!" Lucy exclaimed. "Let's go clubbing tonight. We both could do with it. I've been doing overtime at the shop for weeks too, I need to let my hair down and have some fun."

"That's just what I need!" I smiled. "I haven't got drunk in so long."

Lucy giggled in appreciation. "Let's quickly tidy up the shop so we can go to town and buy ourselves some new outfits. Our shift is nearly over, anyway."

She nodded towards the empty surroundings.

We both got to work, wiping down the surfaces with sanitizer, and cleaning out the coffee machines.

* * *

AFTER AN HOUR, we'd both cleaned up the shop, and we made our way downtown, walking through the shopping center, still wearing our uniforms.

"Which shop should we go to?" I murmured, as my eyes flashed around to the different stores, Next, New Look,

Victoria's Secret, Peacock's, River Island, Selfridge's, and more.

Lucy seemed distracted, and her eyes were fixated on something in front of her. I couldn't quite figure out what she was so immersed in.

"Hello? Earth to Lucy?" I said, waving my hand in her face.

She remained stuck in her trance.

"Never mind the clothes," she drawled, winking flirtatiously at somebody in front of her.

"Why? What the hell are you looking at?" I furrowed my eyebrows as I tried to figure it out.

And then I realized she was staring at a man standing next to a bench, immersed on his phone. He had brown skin, black afro textured hair, dark brown eyes, thick eyebrows with a scar in one of them, a rough, rugged beard, and he was wearing a tight white tank shirt that emphasised his eight-pack. He was also wearing grey sweatpants, and black trainers. He had a black striped tattoo on his arm, which had skulls laced in every stripe.

"He is Daddy as fuck," Lucy drawled.

I rolled my eyes, even though I couldn't help but find myself intrigued about this man. His eyes darted upwards from his phone, and he realised we were both staring at him. A smirk formed on his face.

But he wasn't looking at Lucy...

He was looking at *me*.

I could feel my cheeks burn with embarrassment. I did my best to look away, but before I knew it, he was walking towards us.

"Hey." He smiled, his big brown eyes burning into mine.

"Hey handsome," Lucy replied flirtatiously, biting her lip in anticipation.

The man coughed loudly.

"Actually, I was talking to the girl behind you," he admitted awkwardly.

I jolted, taken aback by the forwardness of his words. Lucy looked annoyed folding her arms, because she'd been drooling over him for the past half an hour. She turned around to face me.

"I'll wait for you in Topshop, babe." She smiled, shrugging. "You may as well see what he wants. Don't be too long."

I nodded, and she walked away, leaving me alone with this complete stranger. I found myself biting my lip in embarrassment, not knowing what I was possibly supposed to say or do in this situation.

He continued to hold his gaze with mine, and I couldn't help but take this moment to look at him properly.

Before me stood possibly one of the most handsome men I'd ever seen.

He had this sexy bad boy look to him; his tight fitted top defined his muscles and his tattoo made him look even hotter.

I felt flushed. The only other guy who could make me feel like this was Lazarus. It was weird how this complete stranger was having an effect on me...and I didn't know what to make of that. It felt wrong to be standing here in front of him, it felt like I should only have eyes for Lazarus. Nothing was happening, but I could feel my insides swim with nerves.

I coughed loudly, wanting to break the awkward silence. Wanting to see what he had to say for himself.

"So, how can I help you?" I mumbled.

He smirked, amused by what I'd just said, even though I had no idea what the hell was so funny.

"I saw you from across the mall, and I couldn't help but notice how beautiful you looked," he admitted, smiling.

I was caught off guard, and I didn't know how to react. I could feel my skin burning underneath his gaze.

"Ahm…" I stumbled. "Thank you."

I scratched my arm awkwardly, feeling my throat suddenly go dry as the scene continued to play itself out.

"Look, I'm gonna get straight to the point," he said, in a deep, raspy voice. His eyes were smoldering with lust. "You're beautiful, and I wanna get to know you. I'd love to take you out on a date sometime."

I let out a sigh. This was going too far now. He was attractive, and he was making a move on me. I couldn't allow this to happen, because I was with another man. I had to take control of the situation and make him aware that I wasn't interested.

"Sorry, I have a boyfriend," I shot back.

The man rubbed his chin, appearing unphased by my response. Like me having a boyfriend didn't even put him off getting what he wanted.

And I didn't know what to make of that.

"Well, he's not gonna be your boyfriend forever." He smirked. "Nothing lasts forever, darling, especially with the fuckboys in this day and age." He laughed. "Besides, he doesn't have to know we're seeing each other. But I know for sure I'd never get bored of you, babe. Once I had you as my woman, I'd never wanna let you go."

I folded my arms, annoyed.

"Excuse me? Are you just here to give me a lecture on my relationship?" I snapped angrily. "Cos I'll have you know, me and my boyfriend are very happy together. Thanks for your concern. Now if you'll move, I've got shopping to do."

This man seemed like an arrogant asshole who didn't know how to handle rejection. I didn't want to stay around him for a minute longer.

He looked a little taken aback.

"Hey, I was just joking," he said. "I respect that you're in a relationship. I'm not about to steal another man's woman away from him. I wasn't raised that way."

My cheeks burned with embarrassment, and I suddenly felt bad for having a go at him.

"But there's no harm in being friends, is there?" he asked hopefully, his eyes glinting.

I scratched my arm awkwardly, not knowing how to rectify this situation.

Friends...?

I could do that.

"Erm...I guess not," I stumbled.

Everything was happening so fast that I didn't even know what to say anymore

"Here, take my number." He smirked.

Before I had the chance to realise what I was doing, I handed my phone over to him, allowing him to tap his number into my keypad and save it into my contacts. This felt wrong, and I couldn't help but feel a little guilty inside. I knew he was just asking to be friends, but I couldn't help but think of what Lazarus would make of this if I told him I took the number of a stranger from the mall.

I pushed my doubts to the back of my head, not wanting to overthink the situation and make myself miserable. There was nothing wrong with having friends, right?

"Okay, thanks..." I mumbled as I shoved my phone back into my pocket.

The man's eyes continued to burn into mine. It was hard to read him. It was like he was a mystery, full of untold secrets.

"I'm gonna leave you to do your shopping, I've got some stuff to do." He smiled, waving at me. "I'll see you around."

He turned, and began walking away.

"Wait!" I found myself calling out to him, the word rolling off my tongue before I had the chance to stop it.

"What?" he asked, turning back to face me. He looked amused, and satisfied with himself.

"I didn't get your name," I mumbled.

He chuckled.

"You'll find out soon!" He shrugged, and then shot me a wink that caused my heart to do flip-flops. I didn't know what this feeling was, but I knew I had better shut it off before I ended up doing something I would regret later.

"That was...weird," I muttered to myself awkwardly. I rolled my eyes, doing my best to play it off as nothing. I began to walk, one foot in front of the other, ready to make my way back to Lucy.

* * *

I MET LUCY IN TOPSHOP, just like we agreed. She was standing next to the high heels rack, looking frustrated and bored.

"I was waiting for you for ages!" she shot at me as she watched me approach. "What did he want, anyway?"

"You can have him," I sneered. "I told him I have a boyfriend, and I'm not interested."

Lucy rolled her eyes, unimpressed.

"You must be hella whipped over Lazarus to turn down a guy as sexy as that," she retorted, laughing. "I know one day in bed with him would be enough for me to forget my own name."

I couldn't help but giggle back in response. I mean, she wasn't wrong. The man was very attractive. I just didn't want to have an affair with somebody and cheat on Lazarus after how good he had been to me lately.

"Anyway, I found some outfits for us to try," Lucy went

on, signaling some clothes she'd picked out. "I've already picked mine, now you choose yours."

She nodded towards the blue bodycon dress that she'd picked for herself. My eyes narrowed across the selection, and stopped when I saw a beautiful pink gown which dipped at the cleavage and had a fishtail design to emphasise the ass. It was beautiful.

I made my way to the changing rooms, slipping into the gown, and stared at myself in the mirror, unable to believe my eyes. I felt gorgeous, and I could feel my cheeks flush bright pink. I smoothed my hands over my ass and my waist in appreciation.

"It looks amazing on you!" Lucy giggled as I walked out of the dressing room to show her.

"Thanks, babe," I exclaimed, suddenly beyond excited to go out with her tonight.

I changed out of the gown back into my ordinary work outfit, and we went to the till to pay for our clothes.

"Let's get out of here," Lucy suggested, and we made our way out of the shop.

* * *

AFTER EATING FAT, juicy, spicy chicken fillet burger meals from the food court, we made our way outside to the car park, satisfied after having a great day.

"Me and the girls will come pick you up from yours at ten o'clock, babe." Lucy smiled as I got into my car, ready to drive home.

I nodded, and then began to drive home, a smile on my face for the entire journey.

* * *

TIME PASSED QUICKLY after watching some television, and before I knew it, it was night. I flicked open my phone to check the time.

"It's nearly nine, I should start getting ready," I murmured.

I made my way to my bedroom, slipping into the gown I'd bought earlier with Lucy, before sitting at my mirror, ready to style my hair and do my makeup.

I allowed myself to do a full beat of makeup, because I wanted to look my best, as I rarely ever dressed up. So I allowed myself to go all out, with foundation, to contour, to false eyelashes and aqua contact lenses.

"I look good!" I exclaimed.

I looked up to check the clock. I still had twenty minutes until the girls would come and pick me up. I had a bit of time to burn at home, then. I told Sophia that I was going out tonight, and then made my way back to my bedroom.

A sudden vibration of my phone caused me to jump, and snap out of my thoughts.

"Why's my phone vibrating?" I murmured. "It's not ten o'clock yet."

I took my phone into my hands, to see that an unknown number was texting me.

UNKNOWN NUMBER: Hey, it's the guy from the mall.

RAVEN: Hey! I didn't think you were actually going to text me.

UNKNOWN NUMBER: Haha, I don't forget a pretty face that fast.

. . .

RAVEN: So what name am I meant to save your number under, or are you just not gonna tell me your name at all?

UNKNOWN NUMBER: I told you, you'll find out soon, babe. ;) All in good time.

RAVEN: Haha.

UNKNOWN NUMBER: What are you doing tonight anyway?

RAVEN: I'm going to hit the club with my girls, I haven't been out for ages.

UNKNOWN NUMBER: Haha, that's cute. I might go to the club myself actually.

RAVEN: Really?

UNKNOWN NUMBER: Yep, I want to go even more now that I know you're gonna be there. Which one are you going to?

I FOUND MYSELF GIGGLING. His comments felt a little inappropriate, but I couldn't stop myself from blushing. He was cute, and he knew how to say the right things.

A sudden creak of my door caused me to put my phone down on my bedside table, as I looked up to see who it was.

Lazarus was standing at my door with a smile on his face.

"Hey babe!" I exclaimed.

"Hey babe." Lazarus grinned. "What are you up to? I thought we could eat and watch a movie."

I scratched my arm awkwardly, feeling a little guilty that Lazarus had already made plans for us, but I told Lucy I would go out with her tonight.

"Sorry, babe, I can't," I apologized. "I'm going out with the girls tonight."

Lazarus rubbed his chin in thought, looking a little annoyed. His eyes burned into mine as he looked me up and down, taking in my outfit.

"Dressed like that? On a night out with your *girls*?" He folded his arms in disbelief, glaring at me with disapproval as he stared at my cleavage.

I bit my lip anxiously, not wanting to upset him or cause an argument, because things had been going so well between us. I did my best to rectify the situation, and lighten the atmosphere.

"Well, we're going clubbing, babe, so I can't exactly go to the bar wearing a bin bag," I joked.

Lazarus rolled his eyes, but his facial expression went back to neutral.

"Whatever, just make sure you don't drink too much and you don't stay out too late." Lazarus folded his arms.

"I won't, babe, don't worry." I giggled, finding it cute that he cared about my safety and wellbeing.

Lazarus narrowed his eyes, as if he were trying to figure out something. I followed his gaze, and realized he was looking straight towards my phone, which was still lying down on my bedside table. My phone was flashing and vibrating repeatedly. I swallowed down a lump that had caught in my throat. It was probably the man I'd met in the mall texting me.

"Why does your phone keep buzzing?" Lazarus questioned, scratching his neck.

"Oh, it's probably one of my girls…" I shrugged awkwardly, wishing he would leave the subject alone because I didn't want to annoy him further.

"Show me your phone," he ordered sternly, his voice cold. He folded his arms angrily, his face folding into a matter-of-fact expression.

"Why?" I asked, my facial expression falling because now he looked angry…

The last thing I could do was *smile.*

"Just fucking show me!" Lazarus demanded.

He moved me out of the way, and picked up my phone from the bedside table. He flicked through my messages, staring at them intently, and then bloody murder was suddenly written all over his face. He let out a blood-curdling scream I watched my life flash before my eyes.

The same feeling I'd had when I'd caught him in the mansion basement.

"Who the fuck is this random guy on your phone?" Lazarus screamed.

RAVEN

"*I*-I can explain!" I quivered. "I met him in the mall today, and he said he wanted to be friends."

"Friends?" Lazarus barked, cracking up with manic laughter. "The guy wants to get you in bed, goddammit! Babe this, babe that. It's as if you want him to flirt with you! You're not stopping him!"

"But I didn't flirt back!" I was mortified.

"I don't fucking care! You're speaking to guys knowing they want to have sex with you! Do you not fucking care about how I feel? Do you just give your number to all the strangers in town who say they want to be 'friends?'"

"Don't be silly Lazarus, of course I care about you!" I pleaded.

"Well, it seems like you don't!" Lazarus roared. "That's why you're going out dressed like that tonight! You're going to see him!" He cracked up with more manic laughter, and I could feel myself tremble. "And to think I believed you for a second when you said you were going to meet your girls."

Before I could comprehend what was happening,

Lazarus's hand shot up and shot straight across my face, giving me a painful smack that left my cheek stinging. I could hardly believe my eyes. Tears spilled down my cheeks, and I couldn't stop them.

"You will not disrespect me again, bitch!" he seethed. "You're not leaving this house tonight. I'm teaching you a lesson for getting on the wrong side of me."

He punched my face, knocking me down onto the ground before clambering on top of me, repeating his torture, endlessly, relentlessly. I could feel my surroundings blur as he continued with his assault, and I faded in and out of unconsciousness.

I couldn't breathe.

I couldn't breathe...

Blow after blow, my vision went hazy. Hazy as I coughed out blood.

Knowing that the life I once knew....would *never* be the same again.

And before I knew it...

Everything went black.

* * *

LAZARUS BEAT ME, and said I'd broken his heart for speaking to other guys.

I was in agony when it was over, struggling to breathe, with bruises all over my body.

I couldn't believe he laid hands on me, after all the times he spoke bitterly about the people who used to hit me.

He did the same. He was just like them.

I wasn't just going to sit in his house like his puppy and allow myself to be disrespected. I needed to leave before he did any more damage.

I allowed my body to take the time it needed to recover in my broken, bloody state...before I would make my plan to escape, and leave this man for good.

I didn't spend my life running away from the monsters in my past just to be trapped with another one...

LAZARUS

I was at the docks, taking care of my shipment responsibilities. It was a hectic day of work, and I had so much shit I needed to take care of.

"Is the shipment ready to collect, guys?" I asked Tariq and Luis, folding my arms

"Yes, boss. The other men are coming soon to load it off the docks."

"Good. Now contact our distro and tell him we need another package of firearms and more marijuana."

"Yes, boss," Tariq obeyed.

"Call Abdi and tell him to order the hit on the Surenos," I warned. "We're taking over their territory."

Luis nodded, taking his phone out, tapping Abdi's number into the keypad.

"All right, guys, take care of what I've asked you to do," I sighed. "I'll meet you later on, so we can come up with a plan to take down the Surenos. Right now, I gotta go down to the police station, and cover up our tracks."

I turned on my heel, ready to drive to the police station.

RAVEN

I made my way to Sophia's room, wanting to make amends with her. I hadn't spoken to her since the encounter in the mansion basement, and she'd been avoiding me deliberately ever since. I'd spent a week in my room, and now, I'd made a recovery. I didn't want to be on bad terms with my sister. Nothing was worth tarnishing my relationship with her, the only girl who'd really had my back from the beginning.

"Have you forgiven me yet, babe?" I asked Sophia, sighing.

Sophia sighed too, shaking her head. "Of course I have. I'm sorry I've been avoiding you, Raven. I just needed time to get my head together." She let out a breath. "I'm your sister. I can't stay mad at you no matter how hard I try."

I did my best to give her a smile, even though my mind was elsewhere, constantly reminding myself of the torture that Lazarus put me through.

"Anyway..." I began timidly, not wanting to waste any time. "I've come to speak to you because we need to leave this house, babe."

"Why?" Sophia asked, confused. "What happened?"

"Lazarus beat me up last week…" I took my head into my hands, rocking myself back and forth, not wanting to relive the bloody nightmare. I did my best to get myself together, and remain strong for Sophia's sake. "I don't want to be here. I need to leave him."

Sophia jolted, shocked at my revelation.

"That prick laid his hands on you?" she shouted. She took her head into her hands, her eyes welling with tears. "He made himself sound so genuine ever since he helped us out…" She trailed off, furrowing her eyebrows. "But the red flags were there when we followed him that day. I'm not surprised he's capable of doing such a terrible thing, the fucking bastard."

She went on and on, cursing him out mercilessly. And as much as I agreed with what she said, it wasn't going to change the fact that Lazarus had laid hands on me. It wasn't going to erase what he did.

"Are you okay, babe?" Sophia mumbled, a timid expression on her face.

"I'm fine…" I shook my head. "But we need to leave before he comes back to the house!"

"But where are we going to go? And what are we going to do about money?" Sophia asked, her face falling as the full extent of what was happening hit her.

"I have enough money for us to get a cheap hotel for a couple of weeks just until I get another job," I muttered shakily. "We'll need to leave town so he doesn't see me around here…so I can't work at the coffee shop anymore."

"I understand," Sophia sighed. "I'll just quickly collect our things."

She turned, collecting our essentials before we made our way out of the penthouse, and out of the city.

LAZARUS

$\mathcal{I}$ was at the police station, doing my best to eliminate all of the evidence on the Manzellas that was already in the police records. I couldn't allow the police to connect the dots between all of the murders and take down our whole operation. I had to be smart and clever with how I played this out, putting false evidence in the place of the genuine ones after deleting all of the dirt that they already had.

The poor bastards in the force were fucking useless…

I'd been a dirty cop for years now, and nobody had ever suspected me of foul play. Nobody had ever suspected me of involvement in anything shady.

And having a good front to the public was the best way to hide my own shit and make fuck-tons of money behind their backs. Running a whole goddamn organized crime circle.

"Right, now I've deleted all the records, I just need to get rid of these files," I murmured as I tapped away on the computer.

I watched the files erase before my eyes.

"All done. Now this hit on the Surenos should go down

smoothly, and none of it will trace back to us." I nodded to myself in approval.

I got up from my seat, and suddenly felt myself sighing as the thought of Raven banged in the back of my head. Irritating whore.

"Now I've gotta go home and make it up to Raven, so the bitch doesn't start acting up again," I muttered to myself, rolling my eyes.

I exited the police station.

RAVEN

*M*e and Sophia were on the train, ready to move to another city far away from London, and start a new life together. It was scary, because neither of us really had a clear plan or sense of direction as to how we were going to manage. But I knew it had to be done for the sake of our safety and wellbeing.

"We're moving to the other side of the country," Sophia breathed, as she stared out of the train window, watching the trees overlap, the hills whizz past, and the surroundings blur around us as the train picked up speed.

"He won't find us now," I reassured her, smiling.

She smiled back at me.

As long as I had my sister here with me…

I didn't need anybody else.

LAZARUS

"*B*abe, I'm home!" I called out as I made my way into the penthouse. I threw my jacket to the side and let out a sigh, needing to fuck after having such a long day at work. "I'm sorry about before, let me make it up to you!"

I expected to hear the trotting of footsteps, or a call back, but all I could hear…was *silence.*

"Why isn't she replying to me?" I murmured, suddenly a little paranoid as to what the hell was going on. I rolled my eyes, certain she was probably in her bedroom just crying and wallowing in self-pity.

Nevertheless, the lack of a response left me pissed off. I made my way upstairs, storming into her room…

Only to be greeted by *nothing.*

I could feel heat roar in my ears, and color drain out of my face in shock, unable to believe my eyes.

All of her clothes were gone.

My heart thumped against my chest as I slowly backed out of her room and made my way to Sophia's, certain this was a misunderstanding. But then I went white as the realization hit me.

All of Sophia's clothes were gone, too.

"Where the fuck have they gone?" I screamed. *"What if she's gone to talk to the feds about what she's seen?"*

I balled my hand into a fist, punching the wall behind me repeatedly, relentlessly, until I heard a bone snap, and blood began gushing out of my hand.

I brought my hand up to my face, licking the blood off of it, my pupils dilating as anger took over my body.

"You're gonna regret crossing me, bitch," I murmured, my voice dropping to barely above a whisper. "I'll find you before your mouth even opens to tell the feds."

I folded my arms.

"This isn't over."

LAZARUS'S MEN

*A*bdi, Luis, Tariq, Lorenzo and Kane were in a heated fight with the Surenos. Bullets were flying, people were getting beaten up, and others were getting taken out left, right and center.

"Where the fuck is Boss? He ordered this hit!" Abdi shouted.

"We haven't got time to think about him, let's just hurry up and finish the ob," Lorenzo snarled, slicing the neck of the nearest man.

All of the Surenos had been wiped out.

"Now we gotta clean up this shit," Tariq sighed. "Abdi, you get rid of the bodies. We'll go tell Boss about the hit." He nodded towards Luis.

Luis nodded back, and they made their way out of the alley.

LAZARUS

I made my way to the security control room back at my base, where all my men were. Axel took care of the security control systems, so I knew he would be the perfect man to consolidate in terms of what I needed.

"Hey Axel," I waved, walking into the room.

"Good to see you, Boss. What can I do for you?" Axel replied.

I sighed in response, feeling pathetic. "I need you to find a girl for me."

"Who?"

"Her name is Raven Emmerdale. She used to work at the strip club, Hope. Bring her boss in, and interrogate him about any places she used to live, if necessary."

Axel nodded. "I'll get straight on to it, Boss. Don't worry about a thing."

I smiled at him, reassured.

RAVEN

*M*e and Sophia had been in the city of Newcastle for a few days now. We were starting to settle in well. We were still staying at a cheap hotel, though.

"I got a job down at a bakery, babe," I told Sophia, as I walked into the kitchen, to see her eating a margherita pizza. "We'll manage just fine."

"That's amazing," Sophia exclaimed. "I'll enroll at the college tomorrow, and start looking for a flat for us."

"I appreciate the support, babe." I smiled at her thankfully. "I still need to let my girls know I've moved away. I'll give us a while to settle in first."

Sophia nodded in response.

"And stop eating all the goddamn pizza! Save me some, you cow." I giggled, pointing my fingers up pretentiously.

Sophia giggled in response. "Here you go," she offered, passing me a slice.

I devoured the pizza, allowing my tongue to savour the taste. I took another bite, then another, then another...

And suddenly felt sick to the stomach, and I had no idea why.

I could feel bile swimming in my throat. I pushed the pizza to the side, suddenly nauseous. Sophia stared at me with a dismayed expression on her face.

"How are you feeling sick over the tastiest pizza ever?" she remarked.

I coughed repeatedly, desperately trying to get a hold of myself. I swallowed some water, wishing it would make the sick feeling go away.

But it didn't.

"I don't know. I'll go to the bathroom and clean myself up," I mumbled before I trudged towards the bathroom, feeling like absolute shit.

LAZARUS

I left Axel's security control room, only to be greeted by Tariq and Luis. I furrowed my eyebrows. They had a stern expression on their faces.

"Did the hit go down as planned?" I asked.

"Yep, we eliminated them all, Boss," Tariq explained.

"Well done, guys," I replied, relieved. "Your wages are about to go up."

They both chuckled. "Why weren't you there, Boss?" Luis asked.

I sighed, knowing I may as well come clean.

"I've been stressed out," I muttered. "Raven ran away with her sister, and I reckon the bitch is talking to the feds."

Luis furrowed his eyebrows. "I doubt she's talking to the feds, Boss. She's scared of you, and she's scared of what will happen to her."

"I agree," Tariq interjected, narrowing his eyes. "She won't say shit if she knows what's good for her."

"You can never be too sure," I snarled. "I've got a bad feeling because the bitch was obsessed with me, and now she's suddenly cleared up and left. This was the last thing I expected her to fucking do."

Tariq looked amused by my revelation. "She's just out there thinking she and her sister can fend for themselves. The minute she runs out of money, she'll run straight back to you. She's nothing without you, Boss."

Luis nodded in agreement. I folded my arms, taking in what they were saying, doing my best to reassure myself and put my mind at ease.

Maybe they were right...

"Hmm..." I murmured.

RAVEN

J'd trusted my instincts and went to the shop to buy a pregnancy test. I'd been vomiting in the bathroom repeatedly, and I couldn't think of any other logical reason behind it. There was no way that I could throw up pizza. It was one of my favorite foods.

I was sure I wasn't pregnant. I was sure I was just travel sick, because we'd just travelled all the way to the other side of the country.

But it was better to be safe than sorry.

I took the pregnancy test, patiently waiting for the lines to appear on the monitor. I needed to put my mind at ease, because I didn't know what the fuck I would do if I was pregnant. I didn't feel ready to have a baby, not while I couldn't provide for it. Not when I was so broken at the moment, and didn't have the energy to look after and love myself, never mind a child. I couldn't be selfish and bring a baby into this cruel world when I didn't even have the means to look after it properly…

I picked up the pregnancy test. Knowing that it would show the result by now.

And then...

I went stone white in shock.

"No...no, it can't be..." I trembled, tears spilling down my cheeks.

I screamed until my throat went dry, and my voice went hoarse.

Screamed until I was blue in the face.

Screamed until I couldn't scream anymore.

It felt like I would never stop screaming.

"Noooooo!"

My suspicions were correct...

I was pregnant.

RAVEN

trudged back to the hotel bedroom, my heart hammering against my chest. Had the world stopped spinning? I was at a loss. I felt like my life was over. Sophia was sitting down on the bed with her arms folded, her face filled with concern and worry.

"Well?" she asked, her face falling. "What did it say?"

All I could do was give her a feeble nod. She let out a deep sigh of frustration, unable to comprehend what was happening.

And before I knew it...

Tears began spilling down my cheeks.

"Sophia, I don't understand how I'm pregnant!" I sobbed, not knowing what to do.

"Well maybe you should've closed your legs," Sophia snapped harshly.

"We always used protection..." I mumbled, but I knew that even protection wasn't 100% effective when it came to sex.

I couldn't breathe. I couldn't fucking breathe.

"So what are you going to do?" Sophia mumbled. "Are you

going to abort it?"

"I can't abort it!" I breathed, shaking my head.

Feeling like the walls were closing in on me.

Unable to believe this was happening.

"That's a life inside my tummy..." I murmured. "That's my future son or daughter."

"Babe, we won't be able to afford to look after it," Sophia pointed out uneasily, standing up on her two feet. "We barely afford to look after ourselves."

She stared at me, her eyes burning into mine. I looked away, not wanting her gaze to meet mine. Because otherwise, she would *know* what I was thinking...

"And don't even think about running back to Lazarus after what he did to you!" Sophia shouted, rattling her fists angrily.

Yep. She knew...

"You should never go back to a man after he disrespects you or lays his hands on you," she barked.

"But Sophia, he's the father of my child..." I whimpered helplessly, my head searing with pain, my whole body burning as I began sweating profusely. "He has a right to know I'm carrying his baby."

Sophia rolled her eyes. "The bastard deserves nothing with what he's capable of," she seethed, her voice dropping to barely above a whisper. "It's like you fucking set yourself up for heartbreak! It's like you want him to hurt you!"

"He's never hurt you, so I don't know why you're complaining," I snapped back harshly.

I knew she was right.

I knew I shouldn't allow myself to be disrespected.

I knew I shouldn't go back to a man who hits me...

But what other choice did I have?

Lazarus had money. He had the means to provide for this child.

The means I didn't have.

The thought of going back to him terrified me. I didn't know if he would carry on with his abuse...

But this was getting too real now.

I had a baby on the way.

A fucking *baby*...

And I had to put them at a priority, even if it meant putting myself at risk.

"He won't hit me if I have a baby inside me. He won't want to," I did my best to convince myself.

Even though I knew I wasn't fooling anybody.

"He's the father of my child, Sophia. He deserves a second chance."

Sophia stared at me with a blank expression on her face, unable to believe her ears. Tears welled in my eyes, threatening to spill down my cheeks, but I did my best to hold them back. I had to remain strong.

I had to...

"I can't believe you!" Sophia seethed. "We just moved across the fucking country yesterday, and you already want to run back to him?"

She stared at me for a long moment before taking her head into her hands, rocking herself. *Knowing that I had already made up my mind, and nothing she could possibly say or do would change it.*

"Do whatever you fucking want, Raven," she snarled bitterly, her voice laced with venom. "But don't come crying to me when he leaves you for dead in a ditch or something."

She rattled her fists angrily before shoving past me with such a force that I toppled backwards. Even my own sister had no respect for me anymore.

My life was over.

My life was fucking over.

LAZARUS

"Any luck, Axel?" I asked, as I made my way back inside the security control room.

"Not yet, Boss. We haven't caught the girl or her sister on any security cameras," Axel explained, sighing heavily. "But I'll keep trying."

I rolled my eyes, disappointed with the news. "Did you bring her boss in for interrogation like I asked you to?"

"Yes, he did," came a voice. I looked up to see her boss stride into the room. He looked like he hadn't eaten or slept in days.

"Are you gonna give me information, motherfucker, or do I have to shoot you?" I snarled.

"Relax!" he replied defensively. "I'll gladly help you in any way I can. The bitch needs to pay, after the amount of money she's made me lose at the strip club."

My face relaxed as I came to the realization that her boss was willing to cooperate. I folded my arms, ready to listen to whatever information he had that could assist me.

"She used to live down in Southampton a while ago," he

explained. "It's quite far from London, so I'd expect her to have gone there since she doesn't want anyone to find her."

I rubbed my chin in thought, pleased with this revelation. I turned to Axel, who was already frantically typing into his computer.

"Axel, check all you can on the data system for Southampton," I ordered. "I'm going to the bar. I need to get laid after all this stress."

Axel nodded to me, and I rolled my eyes.

"Keep me updated." I shrugged.

And then I turned on my heel and headed to the bar.

* * *

I SLUMPED DOWN ONTO A STOOL.

"Can I have a Jack Daniels, please?" I asked the barman, throwing some cash down on the counter.

"Coming right up," he replied, pouring me a glass, and handing it to me.

I gulped it down in one swallow, allowing it to burn down my throat.

"Rum and Coke!"

"Vodka and tonic!"

"Red berry Cîroc!"

I drank drink after drink, needing to get my head straight. Needing to numb this feeling of frustration that kept running through my body.

Needing to put my mind at fucking rest.

I narrowed my eyes as I saw a woman at the bar sitting across from me. She was on her own too. She had long, jet black hair to her hips, big tits, a slim waist, thick thighs, and a huge ass. Plump, juicy lips that would look great wrapped around my fucking cock.

"She's hot," I murmured in anticipation, my eyes never

leaving her once.

Her gaze held mine, and I knew she wanted me just as badly. She made her way towards me within seconds, walking with confidence, her ass bouncing up and down in her tight mini-dress that left little to the imagination.

I was craving her.

I needed her right fucking now.

"Hey handsome." She smiled, her fingers tracing the collar of my shirt.

"Hey sexy." I smirked, my eyes darkening with desire as she continued her assault. My hand moved to the small of her back, tracing circles on her bare skin as I pulled her closer. A gasp escaped from her, and it caused my patience to wear thin. The little self-restraint I had left was about to fly out of the motherfucking window.

"What's a handsome man like you doing in the bar all alone?" she asked, her warm breath on my skin as her lips rubbed against my earlobe.

"Had a stressful day at work," I sighed.

"Stressed, huh?" She took a step back, biting her lip coyly. "I can think of ways to relieve that stress, babe."

"Now you're talking my language." I groaned in anticipation. Her skin burned underneath my gaze. I wasted no time in taking her hand into mine and walking her out of the club, ready to take her home and fuck her until she forgot her own damn name.

* * *

As soon as we got to my apartment, I wasted no time in tearing her clothes off and slamming her against the wall. She was wearing sexy, lacy red lingerie, and it was pushing me over the fucking brink. I tore off her bra, needing to feel her beautiful fucking tits. I took them into my hands while I kissed and sucked on her neck, and she panted underneath me, hardly able to control herself.

"Fuck..." she moaned.

My lips moved down from her neck to her cleavage, before I took her nipples into my mouth, and she began to scream. I allowed my tongue to swirl around her nipples, sucking and nibbling on them as I groaned in pleasure. I fucking loved busty women.

I flipped her around, needing to see and feel her ass. I smacked her ass, hard, causing her to cry out as I tore her panties off of her and began finger-fucking her from behind. She was soaking fucking wet, and it was driving me mad. My pants were already feeling way too fucking tight. I continued to rub my fingers against her clit before I spun her around again, shoving my fingers into her mouth, forcing her to gag on them and taste herself off of my skin.

I couldn't wait any longer. I needed to be inside of her.

I picked her up by her ass, and her thighs wrapped around my body as she furiously unbuckled my belt and allowed my trousers and boxers to fall to the floor. I allowed my hand to wrap around my shaft, working it up and down, getting it ready for what was to come...

Before I plunged inside of her, and crashed my mouth down on hers.

Needing this distraction.

Needing to forget.

* * *

"THAT WAS FUN, BABE," she panted, sweating profusely. She fumbled for her clothes on the floor, doing her best to put them on as quickly as possible, and not overstay her welcome. My chest heaved as I did my best to regain my composure and recover from the mind-blowing sex I'd just fucking had.

"I'll see you around, handsome." She smiled before she turned on her heel and made her way out of my apartment.

I slumped backwards onto the couch, letting out a sigh. I took my phone from the bedside table, flicking through it.

"I should text Abdi about our plans for expansion," I murmured.

I began typing in a text, but a sudden sound of the doorbell caused me to jolt and throw my phone to the side. I furrowed my eyebrows in confusion, suddenly pissed off.

"Who would turn up to my house at this time?" I sneered. "Don't tell me it's the bitch I just laid telling me she forgot to take her knickers."

I laughed, amused, before I got to my feet, quickly put my clothes on, and made my way to the front door.

When I arrived at the door, I was fucking shocked by who I was greeted by, to say the fucking least. I could hardly believe my eyes.

What the hell was *she* doing here…?

More to the point, *what the hell was she playing at?*

I'd been searching for her for days, and now she had the audacity to turn up to my apartment like she'd never left? Like nothing had happened?

"Um, I'll be up in my room…" Sophia said awkwardly, trudging past us and leaving us alone.

Raven's eyes burned into mine. She looked like she hadn't eaten or slept in days, and it served the bitch fucking right. It served her right for daring to fucking cross me.

"What the fuck are you playing at, Raven?" I snarled. "Why have you come back now? I thought you ratted me out to the feds!"

Raven rolled her eyes, folding her arms angrily. "I left because you hit me, Lazarus," she shot back bitterly.

I balled my hands into fists, but did my best to remain calm, because I needed answers. This bitch knew how to get on my last fucking nerve. She knew just how to push my damn buttons.

"Why are you back then?" I barked.

Raven let out a deep breath, shaking her head, looking at loss of words.

"I'm pregnant, Lazarus..." she breathed shakily as tears welled in her eyes.

I jolted back, shocked at this revelation.

Unable to believe my fucking ears.

Unable to believe what I was hearing.

"Pregnant?" I repeated.

"Yes..." Raven mumbled. She stared at me for a long moment before sighing. "I thought we could put our differences aside for the sake of our baby."

I could feel heat pound through my body. I knew I had to play this right, I knew I had to play this safe...in order to fool the bitch again so she wouldn't cross me again.

I had to tell her what she wanted to fucking hear. As much as it fucking pained me to do so...

"I don't know what to say, Raven..." I murmured. "Of course I'll take you back. I can't believe I'm going to be a father." I trailed off, my skin burning. "I'm going to make myself a better person. I'm going to stop lashing out at you and control my temper."

Raven's eyes continued to well with tears as I spoke to her, but I knew this was the right way to manipulate her. She needed the reassurance, and at the end of the day...We were bound by a baby now. She knew she had no fucking choice.

"You don't need the stress," I went on. "I'm sorry, babe. I love you, and I don't mean to hurt you."

"It's going to take me a while to forgive you, but I could never stop loving you, Lazarus," Raven admitted shakily. "I know we've not been on the best terms lately, but you're my world. You mean everything to me. I feel empty without you. I don't want to be without you for another day. I hope we can work things out."

The bitch still loved me. Even after everything I'd done.

And that gave me more reassurance than ever.

"I'm going to make it all up to you, princess." I smiled at her, bringing my mouth down onto hers for a kiss. "Go get ready, I'm going to take you out for a meal to celebrate the baby."

Raven blushed underneath my gaze, already smitten by me again.

The poor bitch had *no idea* what was about to come now that she was carrying my fucking baby...

RAVEN

*L*azarus and I were on good terms again. He never lay a hand on me again. I wasn't expecting it to go well when I went back to him, but I was pleasantly surprised. I was genuinely happy.

It was just like it was when we first met; a whirlwind romance.

Until the day things escalated quickly, and everything was happening so fast.

* * *

LAZARUS TOOK me to a rooftop restaurant in Blackpool. I ate the lasagne happily whilst I watched the views, the calm ocean water lapping against the breeze, and the night sky scattered with beautiful stars.

"Hurry up and finish your food, babe, I want to go to the beach." Lazarus grinned.

"The beach at this time?" I retorted, giggling.

"Yes, babe, the scenery looks beautiful at night."

I giggled again. "Okay, babe."

I took the last bites of my meal before wiping my mouth with my napkin, and getting up on my feet.

"Let's go." I grinned.

He nodded, taking my hand into his, and we made our way down to the beach.

* * *

WE MADE our way to the beach, and it looked just as beautiful as it did from the restaurant. My eyes glimmered in delight as I took in the gorgeous surroundings, feeling at peace and allowing my feet to get covered in sand.

"Wow, it's so beautiful," I breathed.

"You're so beautiful," Lazarus groaned in a deep, raspy voice that caused my skin to set on fire.

I giggled, blushing furiously.

LAZARUS

"*A*nd our little son or daughter is going to be beautiful too." I smiled at her.

I rubbed my chin, suddenly immersed in my thoughts, as I realised the full extent of what was about to happen. I couldn't believe I was about to do this.

But I *had* to. My son or daughter was going to be the heir of my mafia. He or she were going to have to take over when I'm dead. I just hoped the baby was going to be a fucking boy.

Here goes nothing...

"Babe, when I met you that day at the club, I thought you were beautiful." I smiled at her. "When I saw you were in trouble, I wanted to help you. You have a kind heart made of gold."

I bent down on my knees, watching her eyes well with tears.

"Every day you give me reason to fall in love with you again and again and again. I love waking up to your beautiful face every day. I can't wait to be the father to my baby. I know I can be a total prick sometimes, but I'm trying to make myself better for you. I love you."

Raven sobbed uncontrollably, unable to hold back her tears, completely in awe of my words, hanging off every last one. "That was so beautiful. I love you too, baby."

I took out a box from my pocket with a ring in it, opening it and holding it out in front of her.

"Will you marry me, baby?"

RAVEN

*L*azarus was on his knees, holding a ring out that was mine for the taking. My emotions were at an all-time high. I couldn't believe this was happening.

Never, ever did I expect Lazarus to propose to me.

He must really love me...

And I loved him.

It was scary how much I was in love with him. He always knew how to win my heart over. How to say the right things that would have me running into his arms each and every time. I didn't want to know a life without this man. I was so excited for the future.

"Is that even a question to ask?" I exclaimed, my surroundings blurring around me as my eyes fogged with tears. "A million times yes, baby."

Lazarus slid the ring on to my finger, chuckling, before he got to his feet, bringing his mouth down on mine, kissing me with such a force that I could feel the wind knock out of my lungs.

Here was to now ..

To now...

And the *future*.

I was hopelessly and irrevocably in love with Lazarus.

* * *

A FEW DAYS LATER

I PACED AROUND my bedroom excitedly, feeling like a teenage girl again, and Lazarus was my school crush.

I couldn't believe I was going to get married.

Married, married, married!

I couldn't believe I was engaged to Lazarus! Lazarus. The love of my damn life. He had his faults, his flaws, and imperfections, but I loved him. I truly loved him.

"I've already let Sophia know, but I have to let my girls know!" I squealed, suddenly excited at the thought of telling Lucy. "We're gonna have so much fun wedding shopping. They're gonna be bridesmaids!"

I coughed loudly, doing my best to get myself together, and contain my excitement.

"I should speak to Lazarus!" I squealed.

I made my way into the living room, where Lazarus was scrolling through his phone and texting people.

"Hey babe?" I smiled at him.

His eyes darted upwards as he shoved his phone into his pocket to give me his full attention.

"Sup, baby?" He grinned.

"I was wondering if I could start working at the coffee shop again." I shrugged. "I'm getting bored sitting at home all day, and I miss my friends. I want to make myself useful, and earn some money too."

Lazarus rolled his eyes, looking repulsed by the very idea.

"I make enough money, why on Earth would you need to work?" he retorted. "Plus you need to rest, it'll be good for the baby."

I could feel the corners of my mouth form into a frown, disappointed by his reaction.

"But if you're missing your friends, I guess you can, babe." He shrugged, and my eyes lit up with excitement. "Just don't work too many hours."

"Thank you, baby!" I exclaimed, jumping up and down excitedly.

I was so happy.

So, so fucking happy.

I gave him a kiss on the cheek before I ran to my room, ready to get changed for work.

I then rang my workplace, to explain that I had been away for a long time due to personal issues, and needed time off to recover. They allowed me to keep my job, and rearranged a new schedule for me to come in.

* * *

LUCY WAS WIPING down the surfaces. She looked up and her eyes lit up as she saw me. She clapped her hands to her face excitedly.

"Hey babe!" she exclaimed. "Where have you been?" Her face fell. "I missed you. What's going on?"

"Erm…I had some stuff going on," I mumbled quickly. "But guess what, baby! *I'm engaged!*"

Lucy squealed in excitement, unable to believe her ears.

"No way, baby." she breathed. "I'm so happy for you!"

She started dancing, shaking her ass, dropping herself up and down, and I couldn't help but to roar with laughter.

"I'm going to be a bridesmaid!" she screamed.

A sudden voice caused us to snap out of our hype.

"Hey, I'm Casper," a man waved, making his way inside. He had pale skin and dark brown hair, and he was wearing black jeans paired with a black jacket. "Is this shop still open?"

"Well, duh, it says OPEN at the front of the store, braini-ac," Lucy joked. "What can we get you?"

He laughed in response before narrowing his eyes. "How about this beautiful girl with the brown hair?" He winked, and looked me up and down with a predatory regard, and I couldn't help but feel my insides twist with disgust. I folded my arms uneasily, uncomfortable with his comment.

"Sorry, I'm taken," I snapped flatly.

"Taken?" Lucy remarked. "She's engaged!"

Casper rolled his eyes, appearing unbothered by this revelation. "Being taken never stopped anyone from having a bit of fun, did it?"

"Excuse me, sir, but if you're not going to buy anything, I suggest you leave right now," I snapped matter-of-factly, doing my best to put him in his place.

He folded his arms huffily, his face falling, an angry expression written all over him.

"Whatever, you're not that pretty anyway," he shot back.

Casper

You're going to regret curving me, bitch, I thought, seething. *Lazarus's bitch.*

LAZARUS

 was standing outside of the coffee shop, looking through the window, watching Raven and her friend Lucy speak and entertain a man, who had his back turned, so I couldn't see who he was, or what he looked like.

And I was fucking *furious*, to say the least.

I fucking proposed to her, and she was still making up excuses to go out to flirt with other men?

Who did this bitch think she was?

I'm going to teach you a lesson, Raven, I thought, seething.

RAVEN

*A*fter my shift at the coffee shop was done, I made my way home, ready to eat and spend some time with Lazarus. I entered his penthouse, throwing my jacket to the side, and let out a sigh as I allowed myself to relax. I jolted as I saw Lazarus already sitting on the couch, his arms folded, and his legs kicked up, like he had been waiting for me.

Just waiting for me to walk through that front door.

"Where were you, babe?" Lazarus asked, making his way towards me. He had a blank expression on his face, and I had no idea why.

"At the coffee shop, babe." I shrugged, unphased. "I told you already. Why?"

"Why?" Lazarus repeated. "Why?"

He laughed, appearing amused at my revelation. I scratched my arm uneasily, not knowing what to make of this, or what even brought this on.

"Because I went to visit you at work to surprise you, and I looked through the window and saw a man flirting with you…and you were flirting back," Lazarus seethed, his voice dropping to barely above a whisper.

"I wasn't flirting back," I denied, unable to believe my ears and how he'd got things so wrong. "I told him to get out the shop!"

"I'm sick of your lies, Raven!" Lazarus shouted. "Always asking me to go out, to be allowed to do things. And whenever I let you out, out of the goodness of my heart, you go and flirt with other men! Was me proposing to you not enough, goddammit?"

I jolted backwards, mortified.

"Was it not?" he roared.

Tears welled in my eyes. I couldn't believe he'd been so quick to think the worst of me, and jump to rash conclusions. He'd got me so wrong.

So, so fucking wrong...

"Lazarus, you've got it all wrong!" I pleaded. "You can even ask Lucy! She saw me tell him to go away because I'm engaged!"

"Enough of the lying, Raven!" Lazarus yelled, slapping me across the face, knocking me backwards.

Tears spilled from my eyes as I brought my hand up to my stinging cheek, unable to believe my eyes.

He hit me again.

I thought he'd changed.

I really, really thought he had...

"I've done so much for you, and you continue to fail me," Lazarus snarled. "You need to make yourself useful. I've had enough of you playing around with my feelings."

I continued to sob, rocking myself back and forth, knowing that my dreams were being crushed by the second.

Lazarus was never my knight-in-shining armor.

He was a manipulative, abusive, conniving son-of-a-bitch, and I couldn't believe it had taken me so long to see him for who he really was.

I couldn't keep living my life like this.

I couldn't...

"I'm going to have to initiate you into the mafia life," Lazarus said coldly, his voice dropping to barely above a whisper.

"W-What?" I quivered.

"Since you're no use to me at home, you may as well make use of yourself elsewhere," he sneered. "This isn't a choice, Raven. It's a demand."

I knew when he said this he meant business. I knew there was no escaping. I knew this was the fate I was going to have to accept since I'd found out who Lazarus really was.

Being thrown into the dark and dangerous world of organized crime...

"You will pay for hurting me and flirting with other men," Lazarus seethed. "You're going to be an insider of a rival drug cartel, and flirt with the men to lure them into traps, as well as tell me any information you find out. One of my most trusted men will teach you how to fight. You'll also need to get a tattoo on your arm, to show your commitment to the mafia." He trailed off, rattling his fists. "I'll drop you off now."

I was mortified. I couldn't believe what I was hearing. I couldn't believe Lazarus was going to use me as bait, and throw me to the fucking wolves.

This couldn't be happening.

This couldn't be fucking happening...

"B-But w-what about Sophia?" I cried out, my head pounding with worry about my sister, not wanting her to have any part of this.

"What about Sophia?" Lazarus sneered. "This has nothing to do with her. This is between you and me. Sophia will carry on going to college and living a normal life."

A sigh escaped my lips as tears continued to threaten to spill down my cheeks.

Even though my life was at risk...

At least I had the reassurance that Sophia would remain safe.

"Now go and change into something appropriate!" Lazarus snarled, glaring at my outfit. "I'll be waiting for you in the car."

He turned on his heel and stormed out of the penthouse, slamming the door so hard behind him that I yelped.

It felt like I couldn't breathe.

Like the walls were closing in on me.

And now...

I had no choice but to obey whatever was asked of me.

I'd been dancing with the devil for far too long. *They say if you keep dancing with the devil you'll get burned...*I knew he was a monster from the beginning. I should have left him while I still could...but in the words of the monster himself...

Everything happens for a reason, right?

* * *

I CHANGED into a hoodie and some trackpants before I joined Lazarus in his car. Before I knew it, he was driving at high speed down the motorway to his spot.

When we arrived, he took me inside, murder written all over his face the entire time. As I made my way inside, I saw some men working with tech, others who took care of shifting packages, others who took care of accounting and numbers, others who took care of weapons...

There were so many men.

So many damn men.

"This is my spot, where all my men work," Lazarus explained. "I'm going to take you to my most trusted man. He's going to teach you how to fight, and once he's satisfied you can defend yourself, we're going to put you to work and make you the insider of the rival drug gang."

I scratched my arm uneasily, unable to come to terms

with any of this. This felt like something out of a fucking nightmare.

I had to wake up.

I *had* to wake up…

Lazarus rolled his eyes. "Follow me," he ordered.

I moved cautiously, just a few paces behind him the whole time. He pushed his way through more men, more boxes, more packages…until he was inside a room on the other side of the building. A man was standing against the wall with his back turned to us.

He wore a white tank vest, black track pants, and black trainers. He had dark brown skin, black afro hair, and a stripey black tattoo on his arm with skulls laced between the lines.

"This is the man who is going to teach you how to fight," said Lazarus.

And as the man turned around slowly to face us…my heart leapt to my throat.

It was the same man Lucy and I had met at the mall.

RAVEN

J couldn't believe my eyes. It really was him. The man Lazarus didn't have a clue was texting me.

The man who made me feel flushed and flustered.

I hadn't spoken to him since Lazarus had checked my phone that day.

Deep down I was relieved, and felt happiness it wasn't a complete stranger. It gave me comfort knowing I was going to be taught by a familiar face.

Lazarus left the room, and me and the man were alone. I learnt that his name was Damon.

I could finally put c name to the face.

"So you're the chick Lazarus is engaged to," he murmured. "No wonder you never texted me back!"

"Yeah...Lazarus was kinda mad. You're lucky you never told me your name," I mumbled.

If only he knew what mad meant...

"Well, I'm glad I didn't carry on speaking to you," Damon replied, furrowing his eyebrows. "Lazarus is one of my closest friends, I wouldn't want to cross him."

I scratched my arm awkwardly, because what he'd just

said stung me, and hurt me more than it should have. I swallowed a lump that had caught in my throat, doing my best to push my thoughts away.

"Anyway, let's get started," said Damon, smiling. "First, we need to get your posture right. Curl your hands into loose fists, and raise them in front of your face."

"Ahm...okay," I obeyed.

"Make sure your dominant arm is close to your body," Damon explained, "and your non-dominant arm is slightly in front of your body. So, what's your dominant arm?"

"Erm, my right..."

Damon nodded in approval. "Now you need to extend your non-dominant arm forward—so your left arm—but make sure it's not too far forward. This is so you don't hurt your shoulder and pull a muscle."

"Okay..."

I did what he asked, and he clapped his hands in encouragement. I could feel myself burn with embarrassment.

"Well done!" he exclaimed. "You've learnt your posture for fighting. You're a fast learner."

He grinned at me again, and I couldn't help but giggle back. I felt comfortable around him, and felt like I could be myself without having to put up a fake exterior.

"Now, let's put it into practice." He smiled. "Don't worry, I won't punch hard enough to hurt you."

We began fighting each other, one jab after the other, although it didn't really hurt me at all. It felt more like fucking play-fighting, and I couldn't stop myself from giggling.

"Come on, you weakling!" Damon exclaimed. "Put some effort in!"

I rattled my fists angrily, punching his chest repeatedly, doing my best to show him what I was capable of. I punched him harder and harder, but it was like his chest was made of steel, and he was unfazed by what I was doing. Nevertheless, I found this to be a massive stress reliever. It helped me let out all of the pent-up frustration I had inside of me after putting up with Lazarus's bullshit for so long, day in and day out.

The corners of Damon's mouth curled up into a smirk, appearing amused by my attempt at fighting. I took a few steps backwards, before chuckling as I stared at him.

"Take that, sucker." I giggled.

"You're really good for a beginner!" Damon laughed, encouraging me further. "You'll be ready to fight in no time." He gave me another soft punch, which caught me off guard.

"Hey! What was that for?" I retorted.

"What, you thought we were done training after five minutes?" He grinned. "Keep going!"

I rolled my eyes before getting back into my stance, and we carried on practicing for hours. We were laughing together and working up a real sweat, and I couldn't help but find myself getting more and more comfortable with the idea of Damon being my teacher.

* * *

"RIGHT, now we can just work on general fitness, and getting those muscles into shape." Damon smiled after we finished our fighting practice. "Let's go to the gym."

I nodded happily, following him to the gym.

"Now, you can start off with some light jogging in place." He grinned.

I nodded, and began doing what he asked, jogging and working up a sweat. My hoodie clung to my body the more I sweated, and I found myself getting too warm with it on. I allowed myself to take it off because I was wearing a vest underneath, anyway I would just put it back on later.

I could almost see Damon's eyes darken as he watched me take my hoodie off, but I did my best to shrug it off and play it cool, even though his gaze was leaving me burning and making my skin feel like it was on fire. I continued to jog on the spot until I was breathless and needed a break.

"You're so weak and unfit!" He laughed. "How are you tired after a little bit of jogging?"

I folded my arms huffily, not happy with what he'd just said.

"Stop picking on me," I retorted. "It's not my fault I love steak more than I love myself."

Damon continued to roar with laughter, like everything that came out of my damn mouth was just funny to him.

"Don't worry, I'll get you fit in no time," he reassured me, smiling. "Right, get started on some star jumps."

"Okay!" I exclaimed.

DAMON

*A*s I watched Raven do star jumps, I couldn't help but feel my eyes darken with desire as I watched her body move. She was Lazarus's girlfriend…but I would be lying if I didn't admit she was gorgeous.

I hadn't been able to stop thinking about her ever since I met her at the mall. Those beautiful, delicious curves of hers, and her pretty face, with her big brown eyes, her plump lips, her button fucking nose.

I was finding it so hard to fucking control myself. It was hard to, when she was here looking like a million fucking dollars. And she enjoyed my company just as much as I enjoyed hers. The way we were play fighting earlier, the way she giggled at every word that came out of my mouth, the way she hung off my every word and made flirtatious remarks.

If she was so into Lazarus…

Then why would she have a wandering eye? Why would she reciprocate my energy?

Why would she make me feel like she wanted me just as much as I wanted her?

My gut instinct was telling me something wasn't right. That maybe she didn't like Lazarus so much anymore.

But my brain was screaming different. Yelling at me to take my eyes off my best friend's fucking girlfriend. Yelling at me that she was probably just being friendly, and I was mistaking everything she was doing for flirting.

Either way, I knew she needed to stop shaking her ass in front of me before I ended up switching my brain off and losing all sense of my damn self-control. I just wanted to grab her and kiss the shit out of her. I needed to snap out of my delicious fucking thoughts before I ended up doing something I would regret.

"Okay, that's enough star jumps now," I coughed, because I couldn't fucking bear to look at her ass any longer.

"Why?" Raven asked, rubbing her chin. "I haven't even done that many."

"We're moving on to a different exercise," I mumbled.

"Okay," she agreed, smiling and shrugging. "I know! I'll do some squats! They're great for muscle!"

God no, not squats…her ass was going to be poking out again!

I coughed loudly, begging myself to reel in my self-control as Raven started squatting in front of me. I begged my brain to avert my fucking eyes. To look at something else. Anything but her.

But my eyes were fixated on her. She was a fucking work of art. A goddess.

And the crazy thing was, she didn't even realise how sexy she really was. She had no idea the effect she fucking had on me.

"Fuck this shit!" I growled, and spun her around, smashing my lips down on hers before I had time to process what I was doing.

RAVEN

*I*t was all happening so fast.

Out of nowhere, Damon stopped me from squatting, and smashed his lips down on mine. It was so unexpected.

But I didn't stop him.

I should have stopped him. I shouldn't be doing this behind Lazarus's back. I shouldn't be kissing his best friend.

After all, it was Lazarus I was supposed to love...*wasn't it?*

The kiss was full of passion and desire. Like he'd wanted to do it for a long time. I tried so hard to pull back, but I couldn't.

This was Damon, one of the hottest men I'd seen. The man who just had to look at me, and my skin would set on fire. The man who made me lose all sense of self-control, who made my insides twist into knots whenever his eyes burned into mine.

The man who made me feel what Lazarus used to make me feel before he started hitting me.

I enjoyed Damon's embrace. It felt nice and comforting.

I didn't know that something could feel so wrong *but so right at the same time.*

Damon kissed me with urgency, like I was the oxygen he needed to breathe. He slipped his tongue inside my mouth, his tongue playing with mine in a fury. Butterflies were fluttering against my chest, and his hand reached the small of my back to pull me even closer, closing the gap between us.

He traced small circles on my bare skin, causing me to quiver against him as I moaned uncontrollably against his mouth. He let out a satisfied growl against my lips before his hands moved down to my ass, squeezing and slapping it as he picked me up and slammed me against the wall.

My thighs wrapped around his tight, sculpted body, feeling his length rub against my leg, which caused another moan to escape my lips. I could barely breathe as I tangled my fingers into his hair, and he continued to work magic with his mouth and hands.

I had to pull away…

I had to pull away before it was too fucking late...

My mouth parted from his, already feeling at loss of his touch. I felt the sparks and fireworks I'd been yearning for so long after kissing Damon. My eyes burned into his. It was like he was staring right into my damn soul.

I trembled, terrified that this man had such an impact on me. Terrified of the new feelings that were beginning to surface on my skin, throb in my damn heart.

And as I stared at Damon, while our silence deafened the room…

I realized now that I didn't love Lazarus anymore.

DAMON

I put Raven down on the floor, knowing she needed time to process what just happened. Knowing she needed time to get her head together.

But one thing I could say was...

I'd never felt anything like that in my whole damn life.

It wasn't just a fucking kiss. Hell, I'd kissed a lot of women in my life. But it was like she was claiming her soul with mine. And I knew from now I wouldn't be able to shake this woman from my damn mind. I was already having a hard time trying not to think of her...and now she'd given me reason to make her all that was on my mind, every damn day.

I wanted her. I wanted her so fucking much.

I found myself letting out a sigh I didn't know I was holding. I did my best to rearrange my dick so she couldn't see I was erect. She'd left me worked up after that, to say the fucking least.

She was beautiful. So damn fucking beautiful.

Raven continued to stare at me, biting her lip in embarrassment before she broke the silence.

"Erm…" she began. "So, what exercise should we do next?" She scratched her arm awkwardly, waiting patiently for me to answer.

Was she really just going to act like that kiss didn't happen? I couldn't help but to wonder what her deal was. She wanted it just as much as I wanted it. I could feel it, so deep inside of me.

She didn't stop me, even though she's engaged to Lazarus… And apparently madly in love with him. Something just wasn't adding up here. I needed to ask her about it…but not right now. I didn't want her to feel awkward or bad for kissing me. I made a promise to myself to ask her after we were done exercising for the day.

"You can do some weightlifting, and then run on the treadmill for a while," I said, smiling at her. "Then we'll call it a day."

Raven nodded, turning towards the weights rack, my eyes burning into her back as she walked. I immersed myself in my own thoughts.

RAVEN

*A*fter a long day of exercise, Damon and I finally went to the locker rooms to take a much needed shower and change into some fresh clothes, dumping our sweaty ones.

"I'm so tired," I admitted. "I could eat a whole buffet right now."

Damon chuckled. "Don't worry, we're done for the day."

"Thank God," I replied.

Damon's eyes were scanning me; narrowing at the sweat dripping down my body. He looked me up and down, rubbing his chin, seeming lost in thought. I couldn't help but feel a lump catch in my throat as he stared at me. I felt so awkward. I hoped he wouldn't ask about the kiss.

I let out a sigh.

"Raven, what's your deal?" Damon asked, folding his arms.

"Ahm…" I stumbled, "what do you mean?"

"Why did you let me kiss you when you're engaged to Lazarus?" he asked flatly.

I scratched my arm awkwardly. I knew this was coming. "Ahm…" I stumbled. "I got caught in the moment, I suppose."

That was a terrible excuse.

"Raven, I can see right through you," Damon said. "You can't fool me. You wanted it as much as I did." He let out a sigh, taking his head into his hands. "What's going on?"

"Nothing's going on…" I mumbled.

Damon stared at me blankly, his eyes burning into mine. The locker room went eerily quiet for what felt like forever. I had to break the silence, this was too much for me.

"Fine." I swallowed. "I did want it. I don't know if I love Lazarus anymore."

Damon jerked, startled by my revelation, but it left him even more intrigued than he already was. He furrowed his eyebrows, a concerned expression on his face.

"Why?" he sympathized. "What happened?"

I drew out a deep breath, my breathing becoming labored as I looked back on the relationship I had with Lazarus, and it helped me put things into perspective. How blinded I was by my feelings, how I was in love with the *idea of someone* rather than loving them for *who they really were.* Lazarus was no saint. He was the fucking devil, and he ruined my goddamn life. It wasn't love. It was never love. I was just a fucking puppet for him to use at his own disposal.

"Actually, I don't know if I ever really loved him in the first place…" I found myself admitting, wanting Damon to know the truth. Wanting Damon to know I wasn't a cheater or a whore. How could I cheat on a man who was never really mine to begin with?

"He saved me from my boss at a strip club, where I was being forced to let men do horrible things to me," I explained timidly, and Damon's facial expression fell, his eyes blinking with sadness. "I was blown over by the fact that someone wanted to help me. He was my knight in shining armor." I swallowed hard.

"But he was so possessive and controlling. At first I thought it was normal because he didn't want me speaking to other guys, and he wanted me to himself. It's natural to get jealous, but he controlled the clothes I wore, he controlled when I could leave the house. The day you asked for my number at the mall, he came into my room and saw the text messages. He got so mad. He thought I was cheating on him." I stared at the floor.

"And he hit me." I trembled. "He beat me up so badly."

By now, the tears were falling down my cheeks, and I couldn't hold them back. I was tired of being strong when deep down I was broken. I was tired of having to battle my demons on my own. I needed to get everything out. I needed to vent, I needed to make myself feel better...

"He hit you?" Damon shouted, unable to believe his ears.

I guessed there were some things he didn't know about his best friend.

"It made me think if a man really loved me, he wouldn't want to hurt me," I mumbled. "I moved away with my sister Sophia, but then I discovered that I'm pregnant. That's when I came back. I thought that maybe now I had a baby on the way, he would change. And he was nice to me for a while. He proposed to me, and I really thought he loved me." I glanced at him briefly.

"But then he came to my workplace and saw a man trying to flirt with me. He was so mad, he thought I was cheating on him. He keeps getting the wrong idea about me. There's no trust. When I came home, he beat me again..." I trailed off, breaking into fresh sobs. Allowing my walls to break down. Allowing Damon to listen to every. Single. Word. To hear my cries. To hear my cries for help.

I needed fixing.

I couldn't keep going like this…

"I'm so sorry," Damon breathed. "I'm so fucking sorry you had to go through that."

"He said I had to pay for breaking his heart," I whispered. "He initiating me into the mafia life…that's why I'm here. I don't know if I love him anymore. He breaks my heart again and again. I just stayed with him all of this time and did my best to see the good in him because I knew I had no life to go back to. If it weren't for him, I would still be working at the strip club…"

"Just because he did you a favour, it doesn't give him the right to be so possessive and abusive!" Damon snapped angrily. "God, I'm so mad."

Damon wrapped his arms around me, allowing me to sob against his chest. Allowing me to let out all of my feelings, listening to me, not making me feel like I was invalid for feeling this way. Not making me feel stupid. Not putting the blame on me for staying with Lazarus…but seeing Lazarus for who he really was.

And I was so thankful to him for that. As I sobbed against his chest, and took in his warmth…for the first time in my life, *I truly felt at home.*

DAMON

*S*he was so fucking vulnerable.

As she sobbed against my chest, I could feel my heart break into millions of tiny pieces. I couldn't imagine what it was like to force yourself to endure all of that abuse, day in, and day out, because of the amount of manipulation the bastard put her through.

In this moment, I just wanted to help her. She didn't deserve any of this. From what I'd seen so far, she was an absolute gem. She was so, so beautiful with the most amazing face and body. And that wasn't all. She was so fucking lovely, so sweet and caring.

I wished there were something I could do. I couldn't turn back the clock, though. I couldn't erase everything that had already happened to her, how much she'd endured.

I hated seeing her like this. I had no idea Lazarus abused women. If I'd known, I'd never have been friends with that bastard. I would have buried him six feet under the fucking ground for how he treated women.

One thing I did know was that Lazarus was an enemy to me now…and I was going to help Raven get out of this trap.

I was going to help her even if it was the last thing I ever fucking did. She had a terrible past…but that wasn't to say it was too late for her to have a good future.

I wanted to kiss her and tell her everything was going to be all right, but it was too early. I knew she wanted me, but she needed time to move on from Lazarus properly before she pursued me.

And I was going to respect her boundaries and do things on her terms. Not my own. I needed her to trust me.

Deep down, there was a monster inside all of us. We all had our demons. We all had our skeletons in the fucking closet.

But I was going to show Raven that *all monsters aren't evil*.

RAVEN

WEEKS LATER

I stood in the middle of my bedroom getting my head and thoughts together. Lazarus made his way into my room, moving towards me. I folded my arms uneasily, wondering what the hell he wanted from me now.

"Have you been to your fight training today?" he asked.

"Yes," I muttered.

"Good," he said flatly before narrowing his eyes. He looked me up and down with a predatory stare that made bile swim in my throat. "You look really sexy in that outfit. I'd love to pin you down right now."

I rolled my eyes, not wanting to hear any of this fucking bullshit.

"A man has his needs, babe." He smirked.

I couldn't believe he was asking to sleep with me after all the damage he'd fucking done. The man who I used to find so attractive, who I used to be fucking mesmerized by...

Now fucking revolted me.

"Sorry, Lazarus, I'm not in the mood for sex today," I snapped. I knew I shouldn't speak to him like this, but I didn't care anymore.

Lazarus rolled his eyes, unimpressed. "Geez, somebody woke up on the wrong side of the bed this morning," he said sarcastically.

I rolled my eyes again, wishing he would just leave me alone. Me still having to force myself to live with him was bad enough. I'd been training with Damon for weeks now, and it was bringing the two of us closer together. He was such a sweetheart, and he was so genuine it melted my damn heart. Damon was different. I could be myself around him. He didn't want me to change and pretend to be somebody I wasn't. He liked me for who I was.

From the way I burned beneath his gaze the day I met him in the mall, I knew it wasn't going to be the last time I saw that man. And I couldn't help but feel like it was *fate* that brought us back together.

"Anyway, I wanted to ask you something," I mumbled, shutting off my thoughts.

"What?"

"Since I've been listening to everything you've said and been doing my training…" I began wearily, "I was wondering if you could let me work at the coffee shop again."

Lazarus cracked up with laughter, repulsed at the very damn idea, like I was an idiot for even thinking it.

"You've got some nerve asking to go back there after what I saw!" Lazarus accused. "You're staying at home, and you're only leaving the house for your training. Do I make myself fucking clear?"

"Lazarus, you can't keep me locked inside forever," I mumbled helplessly. "If I don't go back to the coffee shop, my colleagues are going to get suspicious and think something's wrong. They might get the police involved. I'm sure you don't want that, do you?"

I furrowed my eyebrows uneasily, knowing I was overstepping the boundaries with Lazarus, knowing I was crossing my damn limits. But I'd already endured so much abuse. I didn't have anything left to fucking lose by standing up to him.

"I guess you have a point," Lazarus sighed.

"O-Of course I do," I breathed, unable to believe he actually gave in.

"Not so fast," he barked. "If you're really going back to the coffee shop, you still have to do your training and all the work down at my spot."

"Understood," I mumbled.

"And you'll have one of my men watching you while you work at the coffee shop," he snarled.

"Is that really necessary?" I denied, furrowing my eyebrows, my face falling.

"Yes, to make sure you don't start flirting with other men again!" he shouted.

"Fine," I snapped, not wanting to argue. I didn't have the energy anymore.

"Good," Lazarus said triumphantly, and then left my bedroom.

I sighed to myself, exhausted. I dug through my wardrobe, flicking through my work outfits for the coffee shop. I threw on the first red-colored coordination I could find.

"This will have to do," I muttered.

I went downstairs.

When I arrived in the living room, I was shocked to see Lazarus standing there with Damon. What the hell was Damon doing here?

"Damon will take you to work today," Lazarus explained,

as Damon stared at me with an intent gaze that caused my skin to heat.

"Okay," I mumbled.

"Make sure you keep an eye on her, Damon," Lazarus muttered. "I've gotta go down to the police station to cover our tracks for the latest shipment."

"Understood, Boss," Damon said.

Lazarus nodded, and exited from his penthouse. Before I knew it, I was following Damon out of the penthouse to his car, and he was driving at a fast speed down the motorway, the wind lapping in our faces.

"I'm glad it's you and not some creep that's dropping me off to work today," I admitted shyly.

He smiled at me reassuringly, giving me the comfort I needed.

"I'm not taking you to work," he said.

"W-What?" I stammered. "Then where are we going?"

"I'm taking you to Crosby beach." He smirked.

I swallowed, not sure why the hell he wanted to go to the beach, but the thought of going there excited me nonetheless. Especially with him.

I couldn't remember the last time I went out. Getting the fresh air I needed would do me a ton of good.

Especially spending it with a man who genuinely cared for me.

* * *

WE ARRIVED AT THE BEACH, and it looked phenomenal. The sun was setting, the sky pink with red tones, the water calmly lapping against the sand. The sound of the waves were so peaceful.

I was in awe.

"It's so beautiful here!" I exclaimed, clapping my hands to my face excitedly.

"It is." Damon chuckled. "But that's not the reason I brought you here."

I turned around to face him, so our eyes were burning into each other. He took my hands into his, giving them a reassuring squeeze, and I could feel my eyes well with tears.

Where had this man been all my damn life?

"Look, Raven, I want to help you," Damon breathed. "I have feelings for you. I know it's a bit fast, and I understand if you don't like me back." He squeezed my fingers.

"From that day I met you in the mall I never stopped thinking about you. I wondered how you were doing, I wondered why you didn't respond to my texts. I'm genuine. I'm not like other men." His lips brushed against my forehead. "I don't care about the job you used to have, I'm not a judgmental person. Hell, I didn't even know Lazarus was a woman abuser.

"What you told me came as a shock. I hate Lazarus now. I want to ruin everything he's ever worked for. I want his world to come crashing down on him. That prick doesn't deserve shit but to be behind prison bars," he seethed.

"I agree..." I murmured.

"Look, Raven, we need to take him down," Damon said. "He needs to pay for what he's done to you. I know I'm no fucking saint myself, being in the mafia business, but it's just a means of survival for me, it's kill or be killed in my world. I grew up in this lifestyle, and it's all I know. Don't judge me for that, baby..."

"The last thing I could do is judge you," I whispered. "You've been so kind to me. So kind..."

"And that's why we need to set him up," Damon sighed.

"How are we going to do that?" I asked uneasily.

"We're going to side with his opposition. We're going to

side with the rival gang he wants you to get intel on after you're done with training."

I found myself rubbing my chin, immersing myself in thought at this revelation.

"We're going to help the rival gang by giving Lazarus false information. When Lazarus goes to the location we've given him, he's going to be leading himself into a trap. Him and any men that have been brought with him are going to get killed by the opposition." Damon drew out a deep breath, taking his head into his hands. "It's a stretch, but we can make it work. If you reckon working with the opposition is too dangerous, we could always just tell the feds the location he's going to instead. Then the feds will know the real truth about what he is, and how he's a dirty cop." His chest heaved. "Either way, we're going to fucking take him down," Damon snarled.

"This sounds like a great plan," I agreed.

He really had planned it to the finest detail. He really was a genuine man. A loving, caring, gorgeous man who had so much to offer. And I'd been so stupid not to realise sooner.

"Thank you for helping me, Damon." I smiled at him gratefully. Letting him know I appreciated every. Single. Word.

Damon drew out a deep breath before taking my hands into his again.

"Any man with a heart would," he breathed. "It's not fair what's happening to you. I like you. I don't care if you don't like me back. I'm happy to be friends with you. I don't want to pressure you into anything. You don't owe me a thing. Anything that happens between us will happen on your terms, not because you feel obligated to…" He trailed off, sighing. I could feel my cheeks flush bright pink as I burned underneath his gorgeous dark brown eyes. My skin was on fire, and butterflies were fluttering against my damn chest.

God, he was so fucking sweet. He didn't want to overstep the mark, he didn't want to make me feel uncomfortable. All he did was care about my feelings. Where did I find this angel?

I needed to be careful, just in case he was only helping me for his own gain too especially after I believed Lazarus was genuine in the beginning. But I severely doubted Damon had an ulterior motive. He was prepared to risk everything for me. He was prepared to go against Lazarus.

He was prepared to risk a damn war.

"Damon?" My breathing hitched in my throat as his name rolled off my tongue.

"Yeah?"

"Kiss me," I whispered.

"Are you sure?" Damon asked, cupping my face in his hands as my eyes glistened with tears.

"I've never been so sure of anything in my life," I breathed, and Damon's eyes darkened with desire. I couldn't wait any longer. I needed his mouth on mine.

He was the remedy I needed.

He was *everything* I needed, and so much fucking more...

The world spun around me as Damon crashed his mouth on mine, kissing me with such an urgency it was hard to breathe. The beach was empty, we had the privacy we needed...

So he wouldn't hold back. He made known how much he wanted me. Every touch he made on my skin, every movement of his tongue, set me on fucking fire. As his tongue caressed my mouth deeper, he groaned against me, and I moaned into his mouth, my whole body quivering. We were just kissing, and I was already so hot for him.

His hands moved up and down my back, caressing my bare skin, causing me to whimper and gasp. His hands slid underneath my leggings, desperate to feel my ass as he squeezed it, letting out a satisfied growl as he continued with his torture. I wanted more, I *needed* more. It was never enough.

I was intoxicated. Intoxicated by him, intoxicated by his touch. I was falling for him.

I needed Damon more than I needed anything in my life.

CASPER

I watched Raven and Damon kissing each other on the beach, and took a photograph for my own damn satisfaction.

Looked like Lazarus didn't have his pretty little toy wrapped around his finger as much as he thought.

He was going to *love* this.

I finally had a reason to piss him off.

I cracked up with laughter, hardly able to contain myself.

Lazarus hadn't heard from me since we were in school. When I dropped the bombshell that his bitch was cheating on him with his best friend, he was going to be so pissed.

Oh Raven, I warned you that you were going to pay for rejecting me in that damn coffee shop.

RAVEN

$\mathcal{M}$e and Damon continued to kiss for a while, until we both pulled away before things spiraled out of control. The beach was hardly a classy place of taking things further, and I wanted the first time I had with Damon to be special.

Damon smiled at me, pressing his lips to my forehead. He had to stop doing that. Forehead kisses were so damn affectionate, it was like he wanted me to fall in love.

Even though that wouldn't be such a bad idea...

"I'm starving." I giggled, lightening the atmosphere.

Damon laughed in response, pressing his lips to my forehead again before he took my hand into his.

"There's a rooftop bar around here, it does the most amazing food." He smiled. "Let me take you there."

"Yes please," I exclaimed.

Damon laughed again before he took me to the rooftop bar, his hand never leaving mine once. I could feel my cheeks burn pink. It was crazy how he had such a big damn effect on me.

"Here it is." Damon grinned as we reached the top of the stairs.

I allowed myself to take in the surroundings, immersing myself...but as my eyes wandered across the room, I saw something terrible. Something I didn't expect to fucking see. I could feel myself go stone-white in shock, unable to believe my damn eyes. My heart leapt to my damn throat.

This had to be a nightmare. This had to be a fucking nightmare...

"Raven! What's wrong?" Damon asked, noticing the terrified expression on my face.

I screamed, unable to hold back the anger anymore.

And then I broke into sobs.

"That's my mum and dad!" I wept.

RAVEN

"*A*m I missing something?" Damon asked, confused. "I don't understand."

"My mum and dad are the reason I had to run away so many years ago. When I was a child, my mum would lock me up without food for weeks and my dad would come into my room and rape me," I explained shakily.

Damon balled his hands into fists, the colour draining out of his face. "Oh hell no!" he seethed. "What bastards! That's made my blood fucking boil!"

I watched Mum and Dad get up from their seats, looking snappy and agitated.

"What's with all the fucking commotion at the front?" Dad barked to Mum. "I want to eat my food in peace!"

"God knows," Mum retorted condescendingly.

Damon was finding it harder and harder to restrain himself. Before I could realise what was happening, he wasted no time in storming over to my parents' dinner table, and began punching Dad in his face repeatedly. Dad staggered backwards in pain, but Damon wouldn't stop. He punched him in the ribs, in his chest, then kicked him in his damn crotch, and I could feel my windpipes constrict in terror as I watched the scene play out. Mum looked horrified, begging Damon to stop. I didn't know what to do.

Damon grabbed hold of my father, who was now struggling on the ground, clutching his body in agony. Forcing him on his feet, Damon slapped his face to the side, and Dad bellowed in pain.

"What is the meaning of all this?" Dad roared.

"You'll pay for what you did to Raven!" Damon shouted.

Dad startled, shocked as my name rolled off of Damon's tongue. Mum looked like she'd just seen a ghost. Both of my parents turned around to see me standing at the other side of the bar, trembling in fear, and began connecting the dots.

"R-Raven?" Mum swallowed weakly.

"Both of you will stop making a scene in the bar and come with me if you know what's good for you," Damon snarled. "Or I'll kill you both right here with no fucks given."

Mum and Dad stared back at him with terrified expressions on their faces, knowing that Damon meant business. Knowing that he knew enough about the two of them to want to put them both six feet under. They obeyed his commands and followed him out. Damon took my hand into his, giving it a reassuring squeeze, as if he were letting me know he was going to take care of this and handle it his own way. I had no choice but to trust him. He was the only person who showed me a grain of genuine kindness in my cruel world.

We made our way to the same beach out back, where we would be able to talk with the privacy we needed. I was still trembling, unable to believe I was seeing my parents after so many years. I hadn't seen them since I was a child, and I wished I hadn't seen them now, either. It was too late for apologies...

Too late for forgiveness.

Too late for redemption.

"Raven, it's been so long..." Dad began with a timid expression on his face. He looked exactly how he did all those years ago, except now, he was older, more fragile, but I bet his sick brain and way of thinking was still exactly the same.

"Oh hell no!" Damon roared. "You don't get to say that to her. What kind of fucking filthy parents are you? Leaving your children without food, hitting them, abusing them?"

Dad drew out a deep breath.

"Raven, I'm sorry..." Mum began, tears pricking in her eyes as she remembered how she used to hit me and lock me away. "It was so long ago. I was on drugs, and I wasn't thinking straight back then. But I'm clean now. I went to rehab. If I could take it all back, I would."

"It's too late for your motherfucking apologies!" Damon bellowed. "Do you have any idea of the fucking damage you've done to her? She and her sister were left alone in the big world to fend for themselves! She got fucking gang raped by members of a cartel and forced to swallow drugs! *All because of you two!"* Damon broke off, seething, and I could feel tears fall down my cheeks as I relived every painful memory. "Not fucking taking care of your children! She had her sister taken away from her for years! She was forced to become a stripper because it was the only way she could make enough money for a basic living! How fucking dare you think saying sorry mends that broken heart? She still has scars from what your husband fucking did to her!"

Mum broke into sobs, terrified at Damon's revelation, looking like the guilt was eating her up inside and about to swallow her whole.

"I'm so sorry, I had no idea!" she wept.

"That's not even the half of it!" Damon roared. "How could you fucking rape your own child? Have you not a human

bone in your disgusting body?" He hurled at Dad again, kicking him in the crotch so hard that he fell to the ground, clutching his crotch area.

"W-What are you talking about?" Mum jumped. "Sure, we were fucked up, but her dad would never rape a child!" She stared at Dad with a sorrowful expression on her face, praying for it not to be true. Praying that she hadn't been sleeping with a fucking child molester.

"Are you going to tell her, or shall I?" Damon roared, kicking Dad again, so hard that he began coughing out blood.

One of the waitstaff ran out of the restaurant, horror etched all over their face.

"I'm going to call the ambulance!" he cried out.

"No, that won't be necessary," Damon snapped threateningly.

"But he's bleeding…"

"No. I don't want an ambulance," Dad barked. "It's fine. I'll be in a lot of trouble if you call anyone. Please, just go away and mind your own business."

The waitstaff furrowed his brows, still darting his eyes to and from us to his phone, sweating profusely, frozen with indecision.

"I said don't call anyone, if you know what's fucking good for you!" Dad yelled through clenched teeth.

"O-Okay," the man stammered shakily, still appearing horrified by the whole thing.

He turned on his heel, and began bolting away from us.

Damon turned back to Dad.

"Well?" Damon gritted, cocking his head to the side. "Spit it out!"

Dad began sobbing uncontrollably. "It's true," he breathed. "It was a mistake. I regret it every day. I'm sorry, Raven." He limped, doing his best to get up on his feet. I couldn't bear to look at him. His face fucking disgusted me, fucking terrified me. It felt like the walls were closing in on me, and I couldn't breathe.

I couldn't fucking breathe.

"You raped your own fucking daughter?" Mum barked in disgust. "How could you! And you kept it hidden from me this whole time!" She took her head into her hands, rocking herself as she screamed. "Raven was telling me the truth that day. I called her a fucking lunatic! I beat her up for accusing you of doing such a thing!"

Dad didn't say a word, knowing there was no redemption now that he'd been exposed for who he truly was.

And now, even his wife didn't love him anymore.

This sorry ass, pathetic excuse of a man.

"Quit the sorry act," Damon seethed. "Don't behave like you did nothing wrong. Luckily for you, I don't hit women. But you better fucking move out of town, far, far away and not show your face round here again." Damon shook his fists angrily as he held eye contact with my mother, who watched her life flash before her eyes. "Because if I see you again after today, I won't hesitate to put a bullet in your fucking skull."

Mum's chest heaved in terror. She shot me a longing glance, as if to tell me that she was truly sorry, but I didn't care. Sorry didn't erase everything she put me through.

She knew now that she'd overstayed her welcome. She turned and began trudging away from us.

"As for you..." Damon breathed, cocking his head to the side to face my father, "you deserve everything that's about to come to you."

He wasted no time in hurling at my father, and this time he was relentless. He knocked Dad to the ground, clambering on top of him, punching his face repeatedly until his jaw snapped and three of his teeth knocked clean out. I had to put a fucking stop to this...

"Damon, don't kill him!" I cried out desperately.

143

Damon took a few steps backwards from Dad, not satisfied that he'd put him through enough torture.

"He's not worth it," I pleaded. "Let him go, and let him live with the mistake he's made every day for the rest of his life. Death is just an easy way out."

I wrapped my arms around Damon from the back, sobbing against him, and Damon weakened beneath my touch, taking his head into his hands. He knew he was going to have to listen to me, since we were doing this on *my* terms...

"You got lucky, old man," Damon sneered coldly, his voice dropping to barely above a whisper. "Now get the fuck outta here before I put your life to an end."

Dad could barely move, but he knew that if he didn't force himself to get the fuck up, he would have to watch his life come to an end. He clutched his body and staggered, slowly limping away from us. Damon turned around to face me, cupping my face in his hands, and drying my tears with his thumbs.

"Shh, baby, they're gone now," he whispered, pressing his lips to my forehead.

"What would I do without you, Damon?" I sobbed. "I feel so broken."

"And I'll try to mend you, piece by piece," he whispered, giving me a soft kiss as our tears mingled together. "No matter how long it takes. Now let's get out of here...in case that motherfucker from the restaurant actually has called the cops or an ambulance."

DAMON

WEEKS LATER

I went down to the spot, where I was meeting Lazarus today for a briefing. I made my way inside, where Lazarus was waiting for me expectantly.

"So, do you think Raven is ready to go into work yet?" Lazarus asked curiously.

I nodded in response. "Yep. I've trained her well."

"Thank you, brother." Lazarus smiled. "I can always rely on you to help me out when I need you. I'll show you my thanks by increasing your wages."

I furrowed my eyebrows, disgusted at his every word, but I had to play it cool. He couldn't know that things had changed between us and I wasn't his friend anymore, or else it would fuck up my whole plan to save Raven.

I let out a chuckle in response. "Thank you, brother."

Lazarus nodded, and then turned and left the building. Whilst he was gone, I took my phone out of my pocket and dialed in Raven's number, needing to speak to her. I held my phone against my ear, patiently waiting for her to answer.

"You have reached Raven Emmerdale's voicemail box. Please leave a message after the tone."

I rolled my eyes, agitated that I'd been sent to voicemail. Where was she, and why wasn't she picking up the damn phone?

"Raven, I've told Lazarus that you're ready to go into work," I said on the voicemail. "Now, we put the plan into action. I'll come and pick you up in two hours, I've just got some stuff to take care of first."

I hung up the phone, shoving it into my pocket, and made my way out of the building, where Lazarus was standing smoking a cigarette and flicking through his phone.

"Hey Boss," I waved.

He turned around to face me, stubbing his cigarette. "What is it, Damon?" he asked, his hands on his hips. "I've gotta go with my men to collect a firearms shipment from the docks."

"I was wondering if I could level up in the Mafia and do a more demanding role," I asked. "I'm kinda tired of just taking care of the security system with Axel."

Lazarus narrowed his eyes. There was a short silence between us, and my heart was pounding against my chest, worrying that I'd blown it.

"All right," Lazarus said finally. "Starting next week, I'll put you in charge of taking care of the shipments. The locations, the number of shipments we're collecting, and all of that stuff. You can also work with Abdi with our plans to expand territory."

I nodded in response, glad that things were finally starting to come together.

"Thanks, Boss, I won't let you down." I grinned.

He nodded and turned away from me, getting in his car and driving off.

I was exactly in the right position I needed to be in the Mafia now. I could get all of the information I needed to lure him into a trap.

"You're going to pay for what you did to Raven, Lazarus Landucci," I murmured.

LAZARUS

*J*parked my car in town and quickly stepped outside for a smoke on the street. It was dark now, and I was pissed off and exhausted with my day to say the fucking least. I grabbed hold of my phone, pressing it against my ear.

"Abdi, I'm running late," I muttered down the line. "I'll be there in an hour."

As I looked up from my phone, I saw a massive shadow looming over me. My eyes darted upwards, and I was fucking shocked at who I saw.

Why the hell was Casper Payper here after all of these years?

That motherfucker Casper. I never liked this bastard, not even in school. I didn't need him wasting my time right now. I had better stuff to do, and more important places to motherfucking be.

"Well, well, well." Casper smirked. "If it isn't Lazarus Landucci."

"What the fuck are you doing here, Casper?" I barked. "Didn't I warn you not to come near me again after we finished school?"

I really couldn't be arsed to deal with this bullshit right now. Just seeing his face was enough to piss me off.

"Why so cold, Lazarus?" Casper seethed, folding his arms and narrowing his eyes, his voice laced with venom. "Are you forgetting everything I did for you? Everything I taught you about levelling up in the game, about pushing more product?"

"Yeah, and you had my respect back then. We were two kids trying to make it on these streets," I shot back. "You lost my respect when you crossed me and helped the fucking opposition."

Casper rolled his eyes, yawning. "That was out of necessity. They were going to put a bullet to my brain. You know how it is out here, brother. Kill or be killed, eat or be fucking eaten. We gotta do what we gotta do to survive."

I stared back at him blankly, not knowing what to fucking say. All of this was so many years ago, so why the hell was he bringing it up and bothering me with it now?

"Casper, are you just here to fucking annoy me, or did you actually want something?" I snarled.

"Actually, I'm here to warn you about one of your closest men," Casper sneered, the corners of his lips curling up into a smirk. "You'll never guess what I saw Damon doing."

"Why should I believe a word that comes out of your filthy mouth?" I seethed, balling my hands into fists.

"Because I want to get back into the game with you, and put our differences aside," Casper stated matter-of-factly. "I have the plug to the biggest distro and connects in the country. You just have to say the word, and I'll tell him to contact you."

I could feel my shoulders tense as Casper said these words. I'd been wanting to expand territory and level up for a long time, taking out any opposition. If what Casper was saying was true, and he did have the plug...

Then it would help me out more than I could have ever imagined.

I narrowed my eyes. Maybe I should hear him out for the sake of business. Maybe this motherfucker wasn't such a waste of time, after all.

"What did you see him do?" I asked finally.

"I saw him snogging your bitch at the beach," he sniggered. "Like, full on lip-locking. They may as well have been sleeping together."

I roared with laughter, amazed at this far-fetched fucking story. Did he really think I believed this bullshit for even one second?

He knew how to make me laugh, I'd fucking give him that.

"Damon's one of my most trusted men. My best fucking friend," I snarled. "He's never ever crossed me. He wouldn't want to get on my bad side over a basic filthy fucking bitch."

"You might not believe me now..." Casper shrugged. "But what if I told you I overheard him telling Raven on the phone that he was going to pick her up in two hours to 'put their plan into action'?"

"What?" I exclaimed, my blood suddenly running cold.

"I'm telling you, they're plotting something," Casper warned. "You have a chance to put a stop to it."

"I'm supposed to collect a shipment from the docks right now," I muttered.

"I'll go for you," he offered. "You go home and find out the truth for yourself."

I sighed heavily, not able to believe this was happening. I was sure the whole thing was just a misunderstanding on Casper's part, but nevertheless, I needed to put my mind at rest. He wouldn't just spin this bullshit tale out of nowhere.

"All right, thanks, Casper."

Casper nodded, and I made my way back to my car,

driving down the motorway as fast as I possibly could, needing to get back to my penthouse and see things for my fucking self. I was just praying that Casper had got it wrong.

But the more I thought about it, the more it made sense. Damon and Raven had been training together at my spot for weeks and weeks. Spending all that time together...

What if they *had* gotten closer?

I shook my head, pushing my foot down on the accelerator.

* * *

I SLOWLY MADE my way into my penthouse, being careful not to make a sound. I couldn't risk myself getting made, and them hearing me walk in.

When I walked into the living room, there was nobody there. This was a good sign.

I trudged further into my apartment, my eyes scanning the surroundings.

And then I heard moaning.

The sound of Raven's goddamn moaning.

I followed the sound. I stopped dead in my tracks as I reached her bedroom door. I peered through the gap in the door...and I jolted in shock, unable to believe my fucking eyes.

Raven standing there, in just her lingerie, tongue-tied with Damon, moaning and whimpering at every kiss, every fucking touch.

Her body was only *mine* to touch. In this moment, I wanted to kill. I wanted to murder. I wanted to wrap my hands around Damon's neck, and squeeze it for all I was fucking worth, making him beg for his life while his lungs fucking failed him.

This couldn't be happening. This couldn't be fucking happening. My best friend...lip-locking my fucking whore.

I couldn't watch this for a minute fucking longer, because I knew I'd end up doing something fucking stupid. I snuck away from the door, and left my apartment, needing to cool off and get my head together.

* * *

I SAT INSIDE MY CAR, my whole body feeling like it was on fire. My head felt like it was going to explode.

I was so angry. So fucking angry.

Damon and Raven were having an affair this whole time, right behind my motherfucking back, and I didn't even fucking notice it...I was blind because of my loyalty to Damon. I never would have suspected the son-of-a-bitch of any foul play. Sneaky fucking bastards.

Raven was going to pay for this. She was going to pay for this bad. Not only that, Damon was going to pay for crossing me. How dare he come between me and Raven? How dare he fuck his best friend's bitch? How dare he take what's mine?

At least now that I knew, I could put a stop to whatever the hell it was they were both planning.

Because now...*I had an even better plan to pull them both apart.*

LAZARUS

*I*t was night, and the apartment was eerily fucking quiet. Raven was asleep, and her sister Sophia was in her room.

It was time to put my plan into action.

I headed towards Sophia's bedroom, stopping dead in my tracks as I reached the door, which was open slightly. I was wearing a mask that covered my face, and a blue Stone Island jacket paired with blue jeans.

I peered through the hole in the door to see that Sophia was standing next to her bedside table, laughing and giggling, immersed on her phone.

There was no more time to waste. I had to make my move now.

I bolted into the room at full speed, punching her head from behind, causing her to fall down unconscious to the floor before she could even realise what was happening. I smirked before I grabbed hold of her body, and began dragging it out of her room, ready to take her to my fucking car boot.

* * *

THE NEXT DAY

I'D TAKEN Sophia across the country, leaving her in a locked room inside an abandoned bunker, where nobody would be able to find her. Kidnapping Raven's sister was the first part of my fucking plan.

I made my way inside of the room, checking to see if she'd woken up yet. She was lying in her bed, and she began to stir.

She rubbed her eyes groggily before she screamed as she took in her surroundings, and leapt to her feet.

"Where—where am I?" she cried out.

I rolled my eyes, amused at how terrified she fucking was. Poor little bitch.

"Nice of you to wake yourself, bitch," I sneered.

She turned around to face me. "Who are you?" she wept. "What is this place?"

I removed the mask off my face so my full countenance became apparent.

She jolted, shocked as she came to the realization that it was *me* who brought her here.

"You!" she accused. "Why are you holding me hostage, you psychopath?"

"I'd watch your mouth if I were you, or you'll end up like your sister," I snarled. "With bruises all over that beautiful body."

She gasped, her eyes welling with tears. "You're sick! Why are you doing this?"

I yawned, getting tired of being around this bitch already.

"Your sister cheated on me with my best friend, that's

fucking why. She needs to be taught a lesson." The corners of my lips formed into a smirk. "Don't worry, babe, nobody will find you here."

Sophia balled her hands into fists, shaking them angrily.

"Why are you surprised that she cheated on you? You hit her, for God's sakes!"

"Shut the fuck up, you irrelevant bitch," I barked. "Nobody cares about you. I bet your sister didn't even tell you about that new boyfriend of hers. That's how much you mean to her."

Sophia clapped her hands to her face, stung by my revelation, and broke into fresh tears.

Drip.

Drop.

Drip.

Drop.

"Yeah, that's right. Cry away, bitch," I snarled. "I don't understand why you defend Raven so much. What has she ever done for you?" I folded my arms, amused. "See, if you came to work for me once you're old enough, I'd give you the world. All the money you need, and a good living. Maybe even have some fun of our own since your sister can't keep it in her pants." I shot her a wink, and she drew back in disgust.

"Don't talk to me like I'm some piece of meat!"

"Whatever," I sneered. "It's a shame you're not going to remember any of what I just told you. You're not going to remember it's me that kidnapped you, or what I said about your sister."

"What are you talking about?" Sophia breathed, her eyes dilating in horror. "Are you going to kill me?"

I cracked up with manic laughter, hardly able to contain myself. This bitch continued to amuse me. She really was nothing like her fucking sister.

"No, I won't kill you," I said flatly. "I have a lot of use for you yet. But when my plan's accomplished, I couldn't care less what happens to you."

"What are you going to do to me?"

"I'm going to drug you up," I snarled, and all that could be heard next...*was Sophia's blood-curdling scream.*

LAZARUS

I'd just finished a shift at the police station, doing everything I could to cover my tracks, and then made some finishing touches which would be revealed later. It had been a long, tedious task. I had to approach Damon, pretending that everything was normal, making small talk with him, and then get some of his DNA by collecting his fingerprints from the equipment.

Phase two of my fucking plan.

"That's all my work at the station done for today," I murmured as I made my way outside. "Raven's gonna be in for a big shock tonight."

I cracked up with laughter.

"I better call Abdi and let him know about Casper joining the Mafia. I can't act like I know what Damon has done. He has to think I'm still cool with him."

I drew out a deep breath before I took my phone out of my pocket, and furiously tapped Damon's number into the keypad.

"Come on, Damon, pick up, you bastard," I muttered as I waited for him to answer.

"You have now reached the voicemail of Damon Walliams. Please leave a message after the tone."

I sighed.

"Damon, be ready at the spot to organise our shipment schedule. Call me back when you get this."

I hung up the phone angrily and rolled my eyes.

RAVEN

*I*t was the first time that me and Damon had ever made love.

And it was amazing. He rubbed up and down my body like I was a goddess. Scars didn't matter to him. He loved all of my perfect imperfections.

His kisses started off gentle and passionate, but they quickly turned rough and needy as I wrapped my legs around him and kissed him back with just as much hunger and lust. He threw me backwards onto my bed, trailing kisses down from my neck to my collarbone, causing me to throw my head back in pleasure, whimpering as he licked and nibbled on my sensitive spot.

He slowly took my clothes off me, leaving me in just my lingerie, and he eyed me up and down like he was an animal and I was his prey. It was so fucking sexy that it pushed me over the fucking brink.

He lowered himself back down over me, and I furiously unbuckled his belt, throwing it to the side as I took his jeans off, whilst he brought his shirt over his head and tossed it. I allowed my fingers to trace his rock-hard chest, every muscle, every beautiful line. His body looked like it had been carved by Greek gods.

I flipped him around so I was on top, straddling his hips, and slammed my mouth back down on his. He kissed me like he'd never kissed anyone before. It was raw, needy, hungry... and full of love.

I couldn't get close enough to him. Every touch left me aching me for more. His hand rubbed up and down the arch of my back whilst I ground against him, feeling his hard length pressed in between my thighs, which caused me to moan and quiver against his mouth as he continued to work magic with his hands.

He took his time with me. Took his time worshipping me. It was like we were fucking each other's souls.

And I loved every second of it.

I continued to moan as his hand trailed up my back to unclasp my bra. He tore it off of me, taking my breasts in his hands, allowing them to bounce freely in his face. He buried his head between them whilst licking them with his tongue, and by now my body was throbbing so much that it ached. He took my nipples into his mouth, groaning in satisfaction as he nibbled and sucked on them, whilst his other hand dug into my ass, squeezing and slapping it, leaving me breathless and struggling for air.

He continued with his torture, moving his hand to my pussy, which was already soaking wet for him. He began massaging and playing with my folds with his fingers, while his mouth never stopped lapping at my nipple, the pleasure of both combined becoming too much to handle. He continued to play with my clit mercilessly, relentlessly, before he moved his mouth back up to my lips and smashed his lips on mine, all while plunging his fingers inside me, causing me to rock against him, my eyes watering with pleasure.

"You're so fucking wet…" he moaned. "So fucking sexy."

He slapped my ass before flipping me around, and lowered his mouth down onto my pussy, licking it from the back like he was a starved man. By now, I couldn't even suppress my moans. They got louder and louder with every lap of his tongue, and it was pushing me over the fucking brink. I needed him inside of me. I needed our bodies to become one.

I knew that after this day, my life would never be the same again.

* * *

BOTH OF US had drifted off to sleep for a few hours. I woke up, yawning groggily, resting my head on Damon's chest as he began stirring and waking up too. He groaned, pressing his lips to my forehead as my hands moved down to his boxers to stroke his length up and down.

"So, when are we kicking off our plan on siding with the rival gang?" I murmured.

"Hopefully tonight," he groaned. "But keep teasing me like that and we're not getting anything fucking done."

"That's a tempting offer." I giggled, withdrawing my hands from his body. We both got up out of bed, and put our clothes on, ready to go about our day. Damon took his phone from the bedside table, and sighed heavily as he read what was on his screen.

"Fuck, Lazarus left me a voice note!" he sighed.

He turned around to face me, taking my hands into his.

"Babe, I'm gonna have to go down to the spot," he sighed. "I've got some jobs to do for Lazarus. I levelled up in the Mafia, but it's all part of my plan to take him down."

I nodded in approval, smiling at him. "I understand, babe, don't be too long."

"I won't, babe. After that, I'll never be able to get enough of you." He slapped my ass playfully, and I giggled in response.

Suddenly, my phone began to ring.

"Who's ringing me?" I wondered. I pressed the green receive button and held my phone against my ear. "Hey, who's this?"

"This is the police," came a voice on the other end.

"The police?" I repeated, surprised. "What's happened?"

"I'm afraid I've got some terrible news," the cop breathed. "There is no easy way to say this."

"What terrible news?" I shouted, suddenly terrified. What the fuck was going on?

The policeman let out a sigh on the other end of the line. "I'm sorry to say, but your sister, Sophia Emmerdale, has been kidnapped. We are doing everything we can to find her."

I could feel my blood run cold as I heard the cop say these words. I was in a state of shock and disbelief. This couldn't be happening...this couldn't be fucking happening...

"What do you mean, kidnapped?" I demanded. "I thought she was at college this whole time!"

"It's too early in the investigation to say what really happened, but we are unravelling some evidence. We have a lead on who might have abducted your sister. We'll stop by your house later on today to speak to you about it in detail."

"What do you mean, you only have a lead?" I roared, trembling. "Work harder! This is my fucking sister we're talking about! Who could have possibly wanted to kidnap her? She was so innocent, she never got involved in anything wrong!"

My whole body quivered. Damon wrapped his arms around me, and I did my best to stop the tears from falling.

"We understand this is a difficult time for you, Miss

Emmerdale, but we strongly suggest you remain calm. There are many possibilities in the investigation. It is highly unlikely that your sister is dead."

I let out a sigh. *Highly unlikely that she's dead* didn't give me any comfort at all. What if she was hurt?

I hadn't been able to protect my sister, the one thing that was supposed to be my main priority in this cruel fucking world. I'd failed her. God knows how she was feeling right now. She was out there, God knows where, and she'd been abducted by a damn stranger...

And that screwed with my mind to the point of no fucking return.

"Okay, I'm sorry for snapping at you," I breathed down the line. "Keep me in the loop on any updates."

I hung up the phone angrily, and now I allowed the tears to fall. My sister was vulnerable, and wouldn't stand a chance out there on her own. I couldn't bear the thought of something bad happening to her.

"Who the hell would want to kidnap Sophia?" I sobbed against Damon's chest. "What if it's someone from the Mafia?"

"Babe, stay calm," Damon soothed me. "We'll get through this. The police will find her in no time and bring her back to us, I promise you. The motherfucker that did this is gonna pay."

I withdrew myself from his body shakily, my eyes hazy as my surroundings blurred around me.

"We're going to have to delay our plans to take down Lazarus," I croaked weakly. "I won't be able to rest until my sister is found safe and sound."

"I understand, babe," Damon soothed. "I'll be here for you, don't worry."

He pressed his lips to my forehead, doing his best to reassure me and make me feel better, even though my mind was spinning with millions of different possibilities that could have happened to Sophia, each one torturing me and etching itself inside of me like a form of motherfucking torment.

"Hey Damon?"

"Yes, baby?"

"Please don't go to work today," I murmured timidly. "I really don't want to be alone right now."

Damon drew out a deep breath. "I won't, baby. Let me just text Lazarus to let him know I won't be coming."

He took his phone out, and began texting Lazarus.

DAMON: *Sorry bro, I can't come to work today, something's come up.*

LAZARUS: *What do you mean, something's come up?*

LAZARUS: *What could possibly be more important than taking care of our shipments?*

LAZARUS: *The shipment schedule is urgent, goddammit!*

DAMON: *I'm sorry, bro, I've got some family issues right now.*

DAMON: *My mum fainted, and I've gotta stay at home to look after her.*

. . .

LAZARUS: *I understand, but your brother Mitchell could have taken care of her instead.*

LAZARUS: *You shouldn't have asked to level up in the Mafia if you can't handle the goddamn workload.*

DAMON: *It's one slip up, bro, it won't happen again.*

DAMON: *I won't let you down.*

LAZARUS: *Fine. I hope your mum gets better soon.*

LAZARUS: *Guess I'm going to have to get Axel to take care of the shipments today instead, then.*

"WELL?" I mumbled. "What did he say?"

"He argued for a bit, but he said he's fine with me not coming today," Damon sighed.

I nodded, letting out an exhalation of air.

"Hey, that's the doorbell," Damon commented, as a sudden sound came from the living room. "The police must be here already. Let's go downstairs."

We made our way to the living room landing. I opened the door, and the cop made his way inside, a stern expression plastered across his face.

"Hello, Officer. Any updates?" I asked.

"Damon Walliams, you are under arrest for the kidnapping of Sophia Emmerdale," the cop barked.

I startled.

Unable to believe my ears.

"You do not have to say anything, but it may harm your defence if you do not mention when questioned something which you later rely on in court. Anything you do say may be given in evidence."

"*I* didn't do this shit!" Damon roared. "I'm being framed for something I didn't do!"

It felt like my world had stopped spinning. Just a few hours ago, me and Damon had made love. And now this was what I was finding out. I couldn't breathe. I couldn't fucking breathe.

Out of all people...I never thought that Damon would be the one to do me wrong. I was too trusting. I trusted him too easily...

And now I'd broken my own heart loving a man who clearly never loved me in the first place. He'd kidnapped my sister. *He'd kidnapped my fucking sister!*

"Damon I d-don't know what to say..." I trembled. "All this time, I trusted you, I thought you were different. It turns out you were plotting against me this whole time!"

"Raven, I love you!" Damon sobbed. "Don't tell me you believe this shit!"

"I don't know what to believe anymore," I breathed, tears spilling down my cheeks.

Damon screamed, grabbing hold of his fists as if he were about to punch the cop in front of him.

"Your fresh DNA was found in Sophia's bedroom after the incident happened," the cop barked, putting handcuffs on Damon's hands. "We can't fault DNA evidence. You need to come with me now."

I bolted out of the room, struggling for air. I couldn't hear any more of this. It felt like somebody was battering at my heart with a chainsaw. Stabbing a million daggers straight to my fucking chest.

I didn't want to know a life without Damon...

And this was what he'd fucking done.

* * *

I PACED AROUND MY ROOM, screaming and crying angrily. Screaming until I was blue in the face, and I wouldn't fucking stop.

I couldn't breathe. I couldn't believe it. I'd never felt so shattered. My heart was aching. *Damon had kidnapped my sister.*

He was capable of lying to me about his emotions this whole time. He never loved me. He was plotting against me all along. A part of me didn't want to believe that Damon could do this. *But his DNA was found in her room.*

He never stayed overnight. He had left, and then come back in the morning. So what the fuck would he have been doing in her room?

My heart was telling me he didn't do it, but my brain was telling me yes.

As much as I didn't want to believe that Damon was capable of doing this, I had to accept it.

He had pretty much been with me most of the time lately...

I didn't quite understand how he even had the chance to kidnap Sophia.

But DNA evidence couldn't be faulted, and I couldn't allow my emotions to cloud what was staring me in the face. As much as I wanted to believe the good in him.

There were times that me and Damon didn't spend together...

So he must have done it then.

There was no other explanation...

After all, everyone who came into my life would just break my heart.

"I hope you're okay out there, sis..." I sobbed. "I love you. I miss you."

I took my head into my hands, rocking myself as I continued to sob. I trusted too easily, and it led to my own downfall. I wished I weren't so gullible. I wished that everything good that happened in my life didn't have to be too good to be fucking true.

As much as I hated to admit it, Lazarus was the only person who could help me now. The police were shit. Lazarus was the head of the Mafia. He had access to loads of stuff.

I needed his help to find my sister.

Trembling, I did the unthinkable. The very thing I never thought of doing, after I'd convinced myself how much I hated this man.

I rang Lazarus.

"Lazarus?" I breathed on the phone, as the line crackled. "I need you."

They say if you keep dancing with the devil you'll get *burned...*

* * *

LAZARUS ARRIVED AT THE PENTHOUSE. Maybe my head was just overwhelmed with grief, which was causing me to act on impulse rather than think things through properly.

But Lazarus was all I had right now.

"What's wrong, Raven?" Lazarus breathed.

"My sister has been kidnapped, Lazarus," I mumbled.

"W-What?" Lazarus stumbled, dismayed.

I took my head into my hands, breaking into fresh tears.

"I'm sorry, Raven," Lazarus sympathised timidly.

"The police came by the house earlier," I mumbled. "It was Damon who did it."

"That bastard!" Lazarus seethed. "He's supposed to be my best friend." He trailed off, furrowing his eyebrows because I didn't respond. He folded his arms, tensing his shoulders.

"Raven, was there something going on between you and Damon?" he asked calmly.

I could feel my heart overwhelm with sadness as I thought back to Damon and I sleeping together, and how quickly things had changed between the both of us.

"I won't lie to you," I admitted shakily. "There was."

Lazarus let out a sigh, shaking his head. "I'm not even mad," he replied with a sorrowful expression. "I reckon he was using you to get to me. It's made me realise what a prick I've been. How I never treated you the way you deserved to be treated. I never deserved you. You were bound to move on."

"Thank you for being so understanding, Lazarus," I mumbled, shocked he was taking it so well.

"But think of it this way," Lazarus said. "Who really loves you? If I didn't love you, would I be by your side right now, despite you having an affair? Would the person you were having an affair with be behind bars? It proves a lot, Raven. I love you with all my heart. You've opened my eyes, Raven. I can't live another day without you."

I broke into fresh sobs. I had no idea what to say to him, no idea what to reply. All I could do was cry.

"Lazarus, will you help me?" I pleaded, trembling.

"Yes, I'll get my men out looking for her straight away," he confirmed.

There was a long silence between us as his eyes burned into mine. I could feel a lump in my throat, and I did my best to swallow it.

"Hey Lazarus?" I mumbled.

"Yes, baby?"

"What about me being the insider to the rival gang?" I asked uneasily.

"You don't need to worry about that anymore. I'll get somebody else to do it. You worry about your sister, and staying calm for our baby in your tummy. There's no point stressing, babe. It's not good for the pregnancy."

"L-Lazarus?" I stumbled, my chest heaving.

"Yes?"

"I'm sorry about the affair," I wept. "I should have never left your side. I thought you didn't love me, that's why I did it...but now I can see how much you care about me. Thank you for helping me. At the end of the day, it's you that's here for me right now...not Damon."

"It's okay, baby," Lazarus soothed me. "Like I said when I saved you from the strip club, I'll help you with my dying breath."

I broke into fresh sobs, my heart feeling like it was about to explode.

"Don't cry, baby, I forgive you," Lazarus whispered. "I love you. I appreciate that you were honest with me."

I didn't know if I should say *I love you* back to him. I felt so confused by my emotions. My heart was playing tug-of-war. I'd spent so much time with Damon that I didn't love

Lazarus anymore. But I had to give him the benefit of the doubt. Even if it meant lying to him about my feelings.

He was all I had, and he was the last chance I had to save my sister.

I gave him a reassuring smile, doing my best to remain strong for my sister's sake.

"Well, remember what I said..." I mumbled. "No more secrets. Remember?"

Lazarus chuckled. "Yes, I remember. No more secrets."

He moved closer to me, bringing his mouth down on mine to kiss me.

And here I was, back where I started.

In Lazarus's embrace.

DAMON

I paced around my cell, screaming and crying as I thought about Raven and the look of betrayal and hurt written all over her face. It etched itself into my memory, and replayed itself over and over like a form of motherfucking torture.

Of course she was going to believe a cop over me, especially when the evidence had been set up to make me look bad. And after Lazarus, she was bound to have trust issues.

But I loved her. I fucking loved her, and it hurt me how little faith she had in me. I would be the last person to do this to her. I'd spent all of my time proving that I was different, that I wasn't an evil monster like the other men she'd had in her damn life.

And this was screwing with my mind to the point of no fucking return.

"I didn't fucking do this shit!" I roared, feeling like I was going crazy. "I bet Lazarus found out about the affair, and he's trying to get back at me. I bet he planted my DNA in her bedroom to frame me. I've never even been in Sophia's fucking bedroom."

I knew it could only be Lazarus who was capable of doing something like this, him being the dirty fucking cop in the Manzellas. And now, he would be using this situation to his advantage, and that made bile swim in my throat to the point it almost poured out all over the damn floor.

I bet he was with Raven right now, brainwashing her and giving her the wrong idea about me...

I drew out a deep breath, doing my best to get myself together. Doing my best to see light at the end of the tunnel, and think of ways I could fix this situation and get myself out of this mess.

I folded my arms, seething, my mind set on vengeance.

"You'll pay for this, Lazarus Landucci," I snarled, my voice dropping to barely above a whisper.

Vengeance is mine.

RAVEN

A FEW DAYS LATER

*L*azarus made his way into the penthouse, looking weary and exhausted.

"Please tell me you have some good news," I breathed.

"Actually, yes," Lazarus sighed. "My men have done a thorough search, and we've found Sophia, baby."

I clapped my hands to my face in happiness, unable to believe my ears.

"That's amazing news! I knew I could rely on you," I exclaimed. "Thank you so much, baby!"

Lazarus smiled. "She's alive and well, thank God. Let me take you to her now."

These words gave me the reassurance I needed. I was so relieved that my sister was okay. So damn relieved.

I nodded towards Lazarus, and followed him out of the apartment, ready to go and see Sophia.

* * *

LAZARUS DROVE ME TO SOPHIA. She was sitting on a bed, her arms folded, looking confused as hell at her surroundings.

"Here she is." Lazarus smiled.

"Oh my God, baby, you're okay!" I sobbed, unable to hold back my tears.

"Why wouldn't I be?" Sophia frowned, getting up on her feet. "What happened?"

"You were kidnapped, Sophia," I mumbled, scratching my arm uneasily.

Why didn't she remember?

"Kidnapped?" Sophia said blankly. "That's weird, I don't remember anything from the incident."

SOPHIA

"She was probably drugged up or something," Lazarus suggested, and Raven broke into fresh sobs. I could feel my heart twist into knots as I watched my sister cry.

"I'm sorry this happened to you, baby. I'm sorry I didn't take care of you or keep an eye on you. I'm sorry I lost focus of what's really important. I'm going to make sure something like this doesn't happen again."

"Don't be sorry, babe, this wasn't your fault," I reassured her, even though I was still in a state of confusion as to what the hell was going on. "You're my sister. I love you."

Raven smiled at me, pulling me in for a hug, and I relaxed underneath her embrace, feeling at ease.

"Come on, baby, let's go home," Raven sighed.

"Who found me?" I asked.

"Lazarus and his men." Raven smiled. "It was so nice of them, I've been out of my mind with worry."

Why would Lazarus find me?

Why was Raven suddenly all over Lazarus again even after how much he hit her?

Why was she acting like he was a saint?

This was so weird...and nothing was making any sense to me.

I decided to shrug it off, and ignore the thoughts polluting my mind. Lazarus left the room, and me and Raven followed suit, ready to go home.

DAMON

 $\mathscr{I}$ paced around my cell angrily. That was all I'd been doing ever since they banged me up in here. Going out of my mind with worry.

With the thought of Raven.

I screamed, getting tired of being locked in this box, when I had so much shit to take care of in the outside world. My patience was wearing too fucking thin.

"How long is it gonna take my brother to come and release me on bail?" I shouted. "I bet he hasn't even found out I'm in prison yet."

I rolled my eyes angrily, until I heard the intercom boom saying, *"Open on forty!"*

The door to my cell opened, and a cop made his way inside. "It's time for lunch," he barked. "Get the fuck outta here, and make your way down to the main hall."

I rolled my eyes angrily, not in the mood for fucking food. The last thing on my mind right now was eating. But I knew it would be no use getting myself into trouble in here, so I obeyed him with no fuss, and followed him to the main hall.

I joined the queue for food, dunking mashed potatoes and baked beans onto my plate before taking my tray over to a table where I could sit by myself in peace without anybody fucking bothering me. I didn't care to speak to anyone, because in my head, I wasn't going to stay here for long.

I started shoving the food into my mouth, forcing myself to eat, because I didn't want to become weak. Before I knew it, another inmate made their way over to me, sitting down at my table uninvited even though I made it clear I wanted to be left alone.

"What's a pretty face like yours doing in jail?" he asked.

"Got accused of something I didn't do," I shot back flatly, not wanting to entertain his dead conversation.

"Aw, that's a shame." He smirked. He looked me up and down with those beady eyes of his, with a predatory regard that made me uncomfortable about my spot. "Your muscles are bulging through that jumpsuit. What do you say, let's go back to my cell and have some fun?"

"Sorry, I don't swing that way," I cut him off, getting more pissed off by the second.

"You dare say no to me?" he roared. "Who the hell do you think you are?"

I cracked up, amused that the stupid bastard had the audacity to pipe up to the likes of me. He looked like he couldn't hurt a fucking fly, let alone someone as well-built as me.

"Oh yeah?" I jested. "What are you gonna do about it, you ugly prick? I'm so scared." I laughed again. Hell, if the canteen had this many jokes, then maybe I should chat to the other bastards in here more often.

The inmate balled his hands into fists, seething.

"This is what I'm gonna do." His fist flew to my face, causing my jaw to swing.

Now I was really fucking pissed off, and my self-control was wearing thin.

But I had to behave myself...

I had to fucking behave myself and take the punches like a pussy, or I'd get nailed for bad behavior and I wouldn't stand a chance of getting out of here...

"You just made a big mistake, you prick," I snarled. "Do you have any idea who I am? I'm secretary head in the biggest drug cartel in London."

"Doesn't matter what you are out there, you're just a prisoner in here," he sneered. "A nobody like the rest of us, doing time. Status doesn't mean shit in jail. You don't scare me."

His words struck a blow to my fucking heart, because the crazy thing was...he was *right.*

And that screwed my mind up to the point of no fucking return.

I was a nobody. A fucking nobody.

And I knew that without Raven...I would feel even more without purpose. Even more alone.

Even more fucking empty.

"Please get me out of here soon, big bro..." I murmured.

RAVEN

"Thank you so much for all you've helped me with the past two days, baby," I thanked Lazarus as he kissed my mouth.

"Raven, I need to talk to you about something." Lazarus pulled away from me.

"What's wrong?"

"Now that we've got your sister back, I've proven my love to you," he said carefully. "And I'm not forcing you to take part in the Mafia anymore. Plus, we have a baby on the way."

"What are you getting at?" I asked.

"Let's get married next week, babe." He smiled. "Now we've sorted out all our issues and life is going smoothly, why delay the marriage any longer? We're still engaged after that day at the beach, after all."

I drew out a deep breath, my heart hammering against my chest. It took me a while to process what was happening, but it was true. We were already engaged, so why delay it any longer? I needed to forget about Damon. He'd betrayed me. Even though my heart still belonged to Damon…my future was with Lazarus now.

I needed some stability in my life. Somebody to take care of my child with me, by my side.

And Damon was in prison for kidnapping my sister.

It seemed like a rushed decision, but I didn't care. All I could think about and prioritise was my unborn baby, and what was best for them. I nodded happily at Lazarus in agreement.

"Let's do this, baby." I smiled at him coyly, biting my lip. "Let's get married."

RAVEN

*M*e, Lucy, and Sophia made our way into town, ready to do some shopping in preparation for my wedding. I needed to buy a wedding dress, and I was so excited.

"I still can't believe you're getting married, babe!" Lucy exclaimed, shaking her hips from side to side.

"Neither can I," Sophia said dryly. She'd been behaving weirdly ever since she found out I was marrying Lazarus, but I decided to ignore it

"I'm going to be a bridesmaid," Lucy sniffed.

I giggled. "Let's go shopping for my wedding dress."

Lucy nodded, clapping her hands in excitement, and Sophia rolled her eyes.

We made our way into a wedding dress shop, where there were beautiful gowns on display and hanging off the railings. White lace, light pinks, lilacs, and more. They were all so gorgeous.

"Go try on some dresses, babe, we'll wait for you here!" Lucy encouraged.

I nodded, taking a few off the rails and going to the

changing rooms in back. My favorite one was a beautiful white gown, with beautiful floral patterns. It dipped at the cleavage and flattered my waist to make it look slimmer, even though it had already been filling out from the pregnancy. It was perfect, just as I'd imagined my dream wedding dress to be.

The groom wasn't the groom I'd planned my dream wedding to have...but I had to keep pushing forward all the same.

I made my way to the girls, twirling around in the wedding dress, wanting to know what they thought.

"You look absolutely ravishing, babe!" Lucy clapped her hands. "Lazarus won't be able to keep his hands off you."

"Yeah, you look so beautiful!" Sophia exclaimed.

I giggled. "Thanks, girls. I'm just so happy right now."

I went to the till to pay for the dress, and had it wrapped specially in beautiful paper and packaged in gift wrap.

"Let's get out of here and go eat some pizza!" Sophia grinned.

I laughed in response. I probably should watch what I was eating a week before my wedding day because I didn't want to look bloated, but I loved food too much to care.

SOPHIA

*M*e, Raven, and Lucy got to the food court, ready to have a big meal after an exhausting day. I had been annoyed all day. I was pissed off that Raven was marrying Lazarus, but I didn't really have much of a say in it. She never listened to a word I said. All I could do was tag along and pretend to be happy for her, when deep down, I was seething that she still wanted to marry such an abusive, manipulative man.

We found a table, and Lucy and Raven tucked into their food straight away. I was distracted by my own thoughts, and I couldn't focus on the food. My eyes darted around the room, and suddenly, my heart dropped out of my chest.

I saw a man standing on the other side of the food court. He was a complete stranger, and I had no idea who he was… but he was wearing blue jeans, paired with a blue Stone Island jacket. There was nothing wrong with his outfit, but I recognized it. I'd seen somebody else wear this exact same outfit before…I was sure *Lazarus* had the same one.

And then my face went stone-white in shock, as the extent of what was happening hit me like a ton of bricks.

Sweating profusely, my memory suddenly became clear. I could remember everything. Everything to the last fine fucking detail. Lazarus had been wearing this exact same outfit that night.

It was Lazarus who kidnapped me!

Oh my God...

Raven couldn't marry him. She couldn't marry such a sick bastard who kidnapped me and then pretended to find me in order to win over her damn heart. I could feel bile swimming in my throat.

I had to put a stop to this!

"Guys, can we get out of here? I'm not feeling that hungry anymore." I swallowed, turning to Lucy and Raven, my eyes watering. I bit my lip, doing my best to stop the tears from spilling even though they were threatening to.

"You sure, babe?" Raven asked, rubbing her chin, furrowing her eyebrows.

I nodded quickly, but I was getting paler and paler. I could hardly stay focused, because it felt like my surroundings were blurring around me.

"Raven, can I talk to you alone for a minute?" I mumbled, scratching my arm uneasily.

"Sure." Raven shrugged. She turned to Lucy. "Lucy, are you okay to wait here for a few minutes?"

"Of course, girl." Lucy smiled. "You girls go ahead."

Raven smiled back at her, getting up from her seat, and we made our way to the public restroom, where we would have the privacy we needed to speak.

"What's wrong, babe?" Raven asked, a confused expression on her face.

"Raven, you can't marry Lazarus!" I cried out desperately.

"And why the hell not?" she remarked, folding her arms sternly, already looking pissed off. "You've had a face on all day."

"Raven, it was Lazarus who kidnapped me!" I shouted.

"Don't be silly, baby, you don't remember anything from the incident," Raven soothed. "I know Lazarus used to hit me, but he's nice to me now, babe. I promise."

"Raven, you've gotta listen to me! It was Lazarus!" I pleaded, wishing she would wake up and listen to me. Wishing that she would see what was staring her right in the face.

"No, it fucking wasn't!" she snapped harshly, cutting me off, completely invalidating my thoughts and my feelings. "It was his best friend, Damon. It was Lazarus who helped me to find you. How dare you accuse him of doing such a thing when you could be dead right now if it weren't for him!"

"B - But Raven!" I begged.

"Enough, Sophia!" Raven shouted. "It's like you can't fucking stand to see me happy. You always want to meddle in things, and ruin things for me, even after I've been helping and providing for you my whole damn life! You're just an ungrateful, pathetic, sorry little girl, and I'm sick to death of hearing you complain all the time. Just mind your own business and focus on college, that's all you're good for. Stop poking your fucking nose where it doesn't belong."

Each and every single word that came out of Raven's mouth stung me like a fucking bitch. It felt like somebody was twisting a dagger straight through my damn heart. She didn't care how I felt. She didn't care about my feelings. All she cared about was herself, and she'd showed it time and time again. There wasn't even the slightest look of remorse on her face after what she said to me.

Lazarus was right. I always defended Raven, and cared so much about her...

When she didn't even care about me.

"Now let's go back to Lucy," Raven seethed. "We can't keep her waiting."

I drew a deep breath, my heart hammering against my ribcage as tears began spilling down my cheeks.

I didn't deserve this. I didn't deserve to be spoken to like this...

When all I was doing was trying to help her, like a good sister would...

She would never believe me.

DAMON

I lay down on my bed in my cell, staring at the ceiling as my mind continued to torture me with memories of everything bad that had ever happened in my fucking life. I was growing weak, and I couldn't take this anymore. Prison was no place for me.

I needed out.

But how?

A sudden rattling of my cell door and the sound of the Intercom saying *"Open on forty!"* caused me to startle and snap out of my thoughts. I rubbed my eyes groggily, getting to my feet, wanting to know what the hell was going on.

And then I was greeted by the last person I expected to fucking see, and I could hardly believe my damn eyes. It was hard to believe I wasn't dreaming.

My brother Mitchell was finally here.

Maybe there was light at the end of the tunnel for me, after all…

Mitchell flashed me a grin, pulling me into a hug and patting me on the back forcefully. "Hello, brother." He smirked.

I rolled my eyes sarcastically, not wanting to give him the happy reaction that would inflate his damn ego, even though I was over the fucking moon to see him at last.

"It took you long enough to bail me out of here," I remarked.

He rolled his eyes, amused. "Come on, let's get out of this dump."

RAVEN

*M*e and Lazarus were in a hotel room, getting reacquainted before our wedding day. I was in my bra and knickers, and he was in his boxers...

I was kissing Lazarus, but the only person on my mind was Damon. I'd spent the last week convincing myself that Lazarus was the right man for me. But I couldn't get rid of my feelings for Damon. I still loved him. I needed to forget him, and I thought that going back to Lazarus would help me do that, but ever since me and Sophia had that row in the bathroom, I hadn't been able to stop thinking about Damon. It gave me second thoughts.

What if what Sophia was saying was true? There was no reason for her to lie. Then again, she had no evidence. Besides, it would make no sense for Lazarus to kidnap her, only to rescue her after.

"I love you," Lazarus moaned, pulling away from my mouth.

"I love you too," I replied, thinking *No, I don't* in my head.

"Ready for round two, babe?" He smirked.

I giggled. "I'm knackered," I retorted.

"I really tired you out, huh?" Lazarus remarked, roaring with laughter.

I rolled my eyes, and he continued to laugh.

"Babe, let's talk about the wedding," I suggested. "It's in a few days, and we haven't even booked a hall."

"Don't worry about any of that," Lazarus said. "With money, you can get a hall booked on the same day."

I folded my arms, amused.

"I wanted to talk about something else," Lazarus mentioned matter-of-factly.

"What's that?" I asked, intrigued.

He drew in a deep breath, like he was about to regret what he was going to say. "Babe, I don't mean to bring up bad memories, but we need to speak about what you had with Damon. He was my best friend, after all."

I scratched my arm uneasily, feeling uncomfortable that he'd brought up this subject. I didn't want to discuss Damon with Lazarus, of all people.

"How did it all start?" he asked. "Was it when he started training you?"

"Lazarus, can we not talk about this right now?" I mumbled. "I just want to focus on us."

"We need to talk about it, otherwise it's just gonna keep bugging me," he shot back. "Did he take advantage of you?"

"No, never that," I replied defensively. "I just got caught in the moment. You were being a prick to me, and he was comforting me about it."

"I can't help but be mad at the bastard," Lazarus seethed. "I can't believe he tried to take what's mine."

"Babe, you don't need to worry about it now. It's in the past," I reassured him nervously. "I'm obviously not seeing him anymore after what he did to Sophia."

Lazarus rolled his eyes angrily. "Did you sleep with him, Raven?" he demanded.

"What kind of a question is that, Lazarus?" I snapped back bitterly.

"I won't be mad at you if you have," he muttered. "I just want to know so we can put the bad stuff behind us, and focus on the good things ahead."

I drew out a deep breath, my heart hammering against my chest.

"Yes, I did sleep with him," I admitted shakily. "But what's the big deal? It's in the past. Besides, I'm sure you've had your fair share of women too."

Lazarus balled his hands into fists, suddenly boiling with rage. He screamed, his pupils dilating as he stared at me with murder in his eyes. I was terrified.

"I'm sorry, did I just hear you correctly?" he stated coldly, his voice dropping to barely above a whisper that caused every goosebump on my back to rise with fear. *"You fucking slept with him?"*

He screamed again, repeatedly, relentlessly, and he wouldn't stop. He wouldn't fucking stop.

My hands leapt to my face in terror as I watched my life flash before my eyes. The monster inside of him was back. In fact, the monster inside of him was never really gone...

"I gave you a fucking home!" Lazarus screamed. *"I saved you from perverted men! I gave you money, food on your plate!"* He broke off, punching the wall behind me as I let out a terrified cry. *"I gave your sister free college tuition! I gave you a fucking child in your belly! And this is what you do to me?"*

"Lazarus, you said you weren't going to get mad!" I wept, pleading with him to calm down.

"I said that so you'd tell me the motherfucking truth!" he roared. *"I can't believe you! I can't believe you'd do this to me!"*

I screamed as Lazarus towered over me. There was only one way this could end. I knew that it was the end of the road for me...

"Time and time again, I gave you so many fucking chances! I've had enough of you!" he bellowed. *"This time you'll pay for real!"*

"Please, don't do anything stupid, Lazarus!" I wept. "You're going to hurt our baby! You're going to regret this!"

"No, I fucking won't," he snarled, and threw me down to the ground, punching me repeatedly, relentlessly, as I coughed out blood and watched my surroundings spin around me.

It was the end.

It was the end of my story…

DAMON

I lay in my bed, staring at the ceiling as the thought of Raven tortured me. My eyes welled with tears as I thought of her. I was bailed out of jail, but still, I had no idea where to go, or what to fucking do to fix this whole fucked up situation.

I needed to speak to Raven. She'd probably been brainwashed into believing it was me who kidnapped Sophia. I needed her to know the truth. I needed her to know that Lazarus framed me.

I drew out a deep breath, my heart pounding against my chest, as I grabbed hold of my phone, furiously tapping in Raven's number. Pressing the phone against my ear, praying that she would pick up ..

Even though deep down, I knew she wasn't going to.

"You have reached the voicemail box of Raven Emmerdale. Please leave a message after the tone."

I hung up the phone angrily, seething. Of course she wasn't going to pick up the call, she thought I was the fucking enemy now. It made bile churn inside of me just thinking of Lazarus using this situation to take advantage of her and manipulate her.

Fuck this shit. I was going to go look for her. I didn't know how long my bail was going to last, so I had to spend my time looking for her. There was no time to fucking waste.

I left my apartment and bolted out to the street, not knowing how I was going to locate her.

But I wasn't going to go down without a fight. I wasn't going to accept this as my fate so easily.

I would die trying before I ever let Lazarus win this war.

DAMON

I took my phone out of my pocket as I made my way down the street, desperately trying to think what to do. And then something ticked off in my head as I thought about Sophia. I was sure Sophia despised Lazarus as much as I did, so she wouldn't believe I had been capable of kidnapping her.

I was fucking sure of it.

I furiously did my best to locate Sophia's number, and then furiously tapped it into the keypad, holding my phone against my ear, my patience wearing thin. She better not send me to voicemail too.

She picked up.

"Sophia, do you know where Raven is?!" I shouted down the line desperately, my eyes welling with tears. "I need to speak to her, please!"

"I think she's at the Disston hotel next to the London County Hall with Lazarus," Sophia replied, her voice cracking. "Why?"

"I'll explain everything later, I've gotta go!" I shouted, and hung up the phone.

I could feel heat roar in my ears as I came to the realisation of what being in a hotel room meant. Lazarus was fucking her to get back into her head and manipulate her.

I felt so disgusted. I couldn't let this happen.

I couldn't let this fucking happen.

She needed to wake up and realise the truth. She knew her self-worth, I'd shown that to her every time she poured her damn heart out to me about how Lazarus hit her. She didn't love him.

She loved *me*.

Except now, she probably fucking hated me, and it was all because of him, that conniving son-of-a-bitch.

I broke into a run, sweating profusely, running as fast as my legs could possibly carry me. I needed to get to her. I needed to tell her how I felt before she ended up choosing Lazarus and shutting me out completely. *I* was the man who treated her like a princess. All Lazarus ever did was treat her like a whore.

I picked up speed with every footstep, making my way to the London County Hall. Then I arrived at The Disston hotel, where Sophia had told me Lazarus and Raven were.

It was time to take control of this situation and fix it once and for all.

DAMON

I made my way up the hotel stairs after threatening the fucking receptionist to tell me which room number Lazarus and Raven were in. I felt bad, but it needed to be done. I was past caring at this point. I was thinking with my heart now...not my brain.

Room 420.

I slammed the door down with a huge force, and then my pupils dilated in terror as I watched the scene play out in front of me.

Feeling my heart shatter into millions of tiny pieces.

Unable to believe my fucking eyes.

Raven was lying on the floor, naked, her whole body beaten and bruised to the core, blood gushing out of her mouth as she tried to speak. Lazarus was towering over her, with his arms folded, murder written all over his face.

"My baby..." Raven croaked weakly.

Lazarus roared with manic laughter. "I told you I'd teach you a lesson for crossing me, bitch! I'm going to kill you! I don't need that filthy child knowing that you're his or her fucking whore of a mother!"

Raven's eyes closed, like she didn't have any fight left inside of her. I let out a blood-curdling scream.

There was only one way to put an end to this shit for good, and that was by doing what I should have done a long time ago.

Putting Lazarus six feet fucking under.

"Lazarus, what have you fucking done?" I roared.

He turned around to face me, his pupils dilating as he stared at me with a murderous expression. Wasting no time, I desperately grabbed my phone and dialled the emergency 999 service. I needed to save Raven.

I needed to save her before it was too fucking late.

"I need an ambulance at The Disston right now!" I roared down the phone. *"Right now!"*

"Ain't no ambulance coming here!" Lazarus sneered, knocking my phone out of my hands. "She deserves everything that's coming to her!"

"You're a sick bastard!" I screamed. "I can't believe I was friends with you! How can you hit a woman? She's carrying your goddamn baby!"

"How can you sleep with the same girl your best friend is sleeping with?" Lazarus snarled. "Wasn't thinking about that, were you?"

"Fuck this argument!" I bellowed. *"I'll kill you!"*

I balled my hand into a fist, swinging straight at his jaw, causing him to lose balance and topple backwards. I clambered on top of him, punching him repeatedly, relentlessly as he suffered underneath my harsh grip.

"D-Damon?" Raven croaked. "Is that y-you?"

"Hang in there, baby, I'm going to save you from this fucking monster," I cried out, my eyes welling with tears. I didn't want to look at how badly he'd hurt her, knowing I hadn't been here for her. Knowing I didn't get here in time to stop it.

I squeezed Lazarus's neck for all I was worth, I continued to batter him. I got to my feet, kicking him repeatedly in his balls, in his crotch, on his motherfucking face. I needed him to feel the pain I was feeling right now. I needed him to suffer for every bad motherfucking thing he'd ever done in his life.

"Goodbye, you disgusting son-of-a-fucking-bitch," I seethed, my voice dropping to barely above a whisper as I grabbed Lazarus's gun from his bedside table, cocking it and aiming it straight at his fucking chest.

"Y-You…" Lazarus choked, coughing out blood. "You h-haven't got the balls to kill your best f-friend."

"Watch me," I snarled, and shot him three times straight to his fucking body.

Wasting no time, I limped towards Raven, clambering over her, my tears falling on her beautiful face, taking her into my arms, pleading this wasn't the end.

"Hang in there, baby, the ambulance is on its way," I sobbed, pressing my lips to her forehead, doing my best not to hurt her. "It's gonna be all right. I'm here."

DAMON

"*She's losing a lot of blood.*"
"*We need to stabilise her condition.*"
"*Initiate life support.*"

* * *

THE DOCTORS PERFORMING emergency procedures on Raven and the way they rushed her into the Intensive Care Unit was all I could think about. The words of the doctors replayed themselves over and over in my head, like a form of motherfucking torture.

I stood with Sophia outside of Raven's room, looking at her through the glass window, fighting for her damn life on life support. And it broke my heart.

"Hang in there, sis," Sophia whispered, a tear rolling down her cheek.

I couldn't bear to look at Raven any longer. I was constantly reminded of my own part in this, how I didn't get to the hotel fast enough to save her. The guilt was eating me alive, consuming me whole.

I trudged away from the area, needing to get my head straight. Needing to think of something else.

Anything but this.

I made my way to the waiting area, and poured myself a cup of water from the water dispenser, still sweating profusely from everything that had happened tonight. A cop made his way over to me with a notepad out.

It looked like it was time for me to be interrogated.

"Hello, Damon Williams," the cop said flatly, folding his arms. "If you don't mind, I've got a few questions to ask you."

I drew out a deep breath, knowing this was inevitable, and there was no point delaying it any longer. I may as well get it out of the way and put myself in the clear.

I needed to stay strong and keep fighting for Raven's sake.

Raven.

The love of my fucking life.

"We found Lazarus Landucci dead at the scene where you called the ambulance." he stated matter-of-factly. "He was a very well-respected police officer. Care to explain what happened?"

I drew out a deep breath.

"He was going to kill Raven," I explained timidly. "He had beaten her up really badly. He had abused her a few times in the past too. I had to step in and save her."

"How did you know where Raven was? Why were you going to see her?"

"I'd just got released from prison on bail. She was the first person I wanted to talk to, and she wouldn't answer my calls. I knew she was angry with me because she thought I'd kidnapped her sister, Sophia, that day. Lazarus Landucci had brainwashed her into thinking I did it."

I took my head into my hands, needing to get it all out, needing to tell the man everything.

"The truth is, Lazarus is a dirty cop. He planted my DNA

in Sophia's room to frame me. This was because he was jealous that me and Raven were having an affair. He wanted to get back at me." I swallowed hard.

"I wanted Raven to know the truth. I asked Sophia where Raven was, and she told me she was at The Disston...so I went there and saw Raven getting beaten. She's pregnant, so I had to kill him to save her."

The cop furrowed his eyebrows, not sure whether to believe the story I was telling him or whether to think it was just utter bullshit. I found myself trembling, wishing my innocence would be proven.

"That's all very well, but do you have any proof of your accusations?" he asked. "How do you know that he's a dirty cop? And do you have proof that he abused Raven? Do you have proof that it was Lazarus who kidnapped Sophia?"

"I know all this because I was Lazarus's best friend," I seethed, doing my best to remain calm and collected. "I stopped being friends with him when Raven told me he was abusing her. Raven can testify to this. Sophia also remembers that it was Lazarus who kidnapped her. She can testify to this too."

"And what about the whole malarkey about Lazarus being a dirty cop?" He folded his arms.

"Lazarus was the kingpin of London's biggest drug cartel. The one that police have been trying to nail for years...the Manzellas. The whole cop thing was to cover his tracks and get away with all the wrong he was doing. If you don't believe me, you can look in your database. Check for deleted records, and files that suddenly "went missing." They were all deleted by Lazarus." I shook my head. "That's not all. If you're not able to find anything, I can literally give you the names and details of everybody involved in the operations, the locations of the hideouts, the shipment ports. I know everything."

And I was willing to leave everything behind for Raven's sake.

The cop shuddered, his tense shoulders relaxing. I knew now that he believed me, and he was willing to let me go free as long as I cooperated.

"If all of this is true, then you have just killed London's most wanted criminal," he murmured. "I'm going to go back to the station to see if all the information you just told me checks out. I have a feeling that you're telling the truth." He let out a sigh. "What you did was admirable. You saved a pregnant lady and gave her justice from her abuse. All your criminal charges will be dropped, effective immediately, and you have earnt the respect of the police in this town."

"Thank you for your cooperation, Officer," I said thankfully, shaking his hand.

The cop nodded left for the station.

DAMON

LATER THAT NIGHT

J made my way to Raven's hospital bed. I hadn't been able to leave the hospital, I didn't want to leave her side for a second after seeing the state that she was in.

She was lying on the bed with her eyes closed. Her heart rate monitor was beeping more calmly now, which gave me some reassurance that she was going to be okay.

But deep down, I was still fucking terrified. I didn't know how I was going to live without her if anything happened to her. I really hoped they would be able to save the baby, too.

"I'm so sorry that this happened to you, baby," I murmured, squeezing her hand, pressing my lips against her fingers. "I went out of my mind in jail thinking about you. I love you, Raven. I love you so fucking much it hurts."

I drew a deep breath, trembling as I begged her to stay strong.

"Please don't quit on me now. Keep fighting, and stay in there. You and the baby are going to be just fine. I'm going to take care of you and Sophia with all my heart, and look after the baby as if it were my own. I'm sorry you got the wrong end of the stick about the whole police and DNA thing. I'm in the clear with the police now, and they've proven Lazarus was behind everything. You can trust me, baby. I'd never do anything to hurt you." I trailed off, a tear rolling down my cheek. "Don't leave me Raven. I love you."

I continued to stare at her, my beautiful, beautiful girl. After everything she'd been through, she deserved a happily ever after.

A happily ever after with me.

A man who would treat her like the queen she was, and not let her be sad for another goddamn day in her life.

And as if by magic...

She started to stir.

I couldn't believe my eyes. My eyes filled with tears of happiness.

She was going to pull through.

She was going to make it.

Her eyes fluttered open, and she brought her hand up to my face, wiping the tears from my eyes. My heart felt like it was going to explode.

I couldn't believe it...

"Oh my God, you're awake," I breathed, kissing her hands repeatedly. "After the amount of pain you put me through, I might as well start going to church."

Raven giggled, doing her best to move her body to sit up, but without success.

"Shhh, it's okay, baby," I soothed. "You need to rest."

"Don't be silly, Damon, I'm fine," she replied, but she did as she was told.

I pressed my lips to her forehead, not wanting to spend another day without this phenomenal woman in my life.

"Oh, and Damon?" Raven smiled.

"Yes, baby?"

"I heard every word you said, you wet mop," she giggled.

I scratched my neck, flushing with embarrassment. She continued to giggle uncontrollably. I coughed loudly, doing my best to explain myself.

"I'll have you know I was expressing my feelings," I remarked.

"It was cute." She giggled. "I love you, Damon."

"I love you too, baby girl."

RAVEN

onths later, Damon and I got married, and I gave birth to the most beautiful baby. He adored it and looked after the baby as if it were his own.

I'd finally got my happily ever after.

"Let's go on to the vows, shall we?" said the vicar, smiling as Damon took my hand into his, squeezing it.

Our big day.

When we would finally be husband and wife.

"Do you, Raven, promise to be Damon's friend, to comfort him, and to listen to him? To celebrate his successes and support his struggles? To love him, respect him, and tenderly care for him, through all the days of your life?"

"I do."

"Do you, Damon, take Raven to be your wife, to have and to hold, from this day forward? For better, for worse, for richer, for poorer, in sickness and in health, to love and to cherish, till death do you part?"

"I do."

"You may now kiss the bride."

"I'll do more than just kiss her." Damon smirked, and pulled me towards him as I giggled beneath his touch, feeling like a teenager again with a school crush. This man gave me new reasons to fall in love with him all over again every single day.

I was no longer Raven Emmerdale. My abused life was something that was in the past.

I'd gained closure. I'd spoken to my parents, and Lazarus was now six feet under the ground for what he did to me.

I was no longer the weak, timid girl I was before, who didn't know how to defend herself.

I was now Raven Walliams. With a new second name came a new chapter in my life.

I may have started off life rough, but with Damon I found a new light, a new purpose.

He looked after Lazarus's child as if it were his own.

And we had two more beautiful babies of our own, a beautiful baby girl and a beautiful baby boy I was currently carrying in my tummy.

After we got married, me, Damon, and my sister moved to New York. Far, far away from London. It was a new beginning for us.

My stripper boss wouldn't be able to find me, nor any of my past enemies. It was a fresh start, and I was happy at last.

I was crazy in love with Damon, and he loved me all the way back.

I finally got my happily ever after.

My knight in shining armor wasn't the man who saved me from the strip club.

It was the man I married, who taught me how to love when the whole world was against me.

Who taught me that my past didn't dictate my future.

Who taught me that life is what you make it.

Who made me realise my self-worth.

Who made me feel like a princess.

And I loved him, my sister, and my children with every breath I took.

* * *

"Let's put the babies to bed." Damon smiled as he cooed to our beautiful little girl in his arms, rocking her gently.

I nodded as I cooed to our other baby. We made our way to the cots, and gently placed them in there, giving them soft kisses on the forehead to wish them goodnight.

Now that the babies were asleep, we finally had some time to ourselves. Damon made his way towards me, closing the gap between us, his eyes darkening with desire as he drunk me in, in my pink maternity dress and my flip-flops.

"Have I ever told you how sexy you look pregnant?" he groaned, eyeing me up and down with appreciation.

I giggled. "Come here."

Pregnancy had my hormones raging, and I wanted to jump Damon's bones every time I fucking laid eyes on him. I crashed my mouth down on his, kissing him hungrily, slipping my tongue into his mouth as he groaned against me, grabbing my ass and pushing me even closer to him. His lips travelled down from my mouth to my neck, causing me to moan and whimper while he slipped his hands underneath my top and began twisting on my nipples.

But suddenly...

I felt weak at the knees, and started staggering in pain.

"What's wrong, baby?" Damon called out, pulling backwards in shock as I clutched my belly.

"I think my water just broke..."

Don't miss the next books in the series:

MORE BOOKS BY A. G. KHALIQ

Mafia Kingpin Duet

Mafia Kingpin Part 1

Mafia Kingpin Part 2

Mafia Kingpin Boxset

Beauty and the Beast Series

Beauty and the Beast Part 1

Beauty and the Beast Part 2

Beauty and the Beast Part 3

Beauty and the Beast Boxset

His Captive Series

His Captive Part 1

His Captive Part 2

His Captive Part 3

His Captive Boxset

Coming soon with Limitless Publishing

Corrupt Me Series

Dangerous Desires Part 1

Dangerous Desires Part 2

Forbidden Fruit

Married to the Mafia Series

Stripped

Capo

ABOUT THE AUTHOR

A. G. Khaliq is a 22-year old upcoming author, residing in the United Kingdom, who struck a publishing deal with Limitless Publishing after garnering almost 3 million reads for her stories on Episode Interactive, an animated fiction 'choose your path' app. Writing sexy and completely badass mafia stories is her speciality.

Goodreads: https://www.goodreads.com/author/show/16955499.A_G_Khaliq

BEFORE YOU GO...

Would you like to be a part of our *FREEBIE FRIDAY LIST* and get **6 FREE eBooks** and other *exclusive* sales sent to your inbox every Friday?

One email every week packed with bookish goodies!

We send out different genres such as Romance, Suspense, Thriller, Westerns, Paranormal, New Adult, and much more! If you'd like to join over 53,000+ subscribers, click below to be a part of FREEBIE FRIDAY...

Join FREEBIE FRIDAY!

BECOME A BOOKSHARK!

Who doesn't love a good eBook bargain?

Now, imagine receiving daily eBook sales straight to your inbox...*Bookworm heaven*!

Sign up for the ***BOOKSHARK NEWSLETTER*** and don't miss out on epic eBook sales ever again!

BECOME A BOOKSHARK